Echoes of The Deep

Lyra Desimone

Published by Lyra Desimone, 2024.

ECHOES OF THE DEEP

First edition. August 12, 2024.

ISBN: 979-8227893826

Written by Lyra Desimone.

Also by Lyra Desimone

Fugitive Echoes
Echoes of The Deep

Chapter 1: The Distress Call

Overlooking the horizon, the first rays of dawn painted the heavens in pink and yellow. Usually a hive of activity, the Coast Guard command center was enveloped in an odd silence. The day shift was just starting to trickle in as the night shift wound down. Captain Olivia Raines stood at her position in this transitional area between night and day, her sharp eyes glancing over the monitors before her.

Olivia was a woman shaped by the sea and polished during years of service. Her weathered face showed the marks of many missions, each wrinkle evidence of her relentless commitment. Not one strand out of place, her salt-and-pepper hair was tied back in a tight bun. She moved with a calm power, her mere presence inspiring respect from everyone around.

Olivia's thoughts were already running over the day's chores as she drank her morning coffee. The bitter liquid provided a sharp contrast to the day's brightness. She looked over the night shift's usual reports, her seasoned eyes quickly spotting any irregularities. It felt as if it would be another typical day of coastal patrolling.

But in Olivia's field of work, average could become remarkable in the space of a few seconds.

The peace of the morning broke with an unexpected radio crackle. A terrified and desperate voice tore over the speakers. "Mayday, mayday! This is the luxury yacht Seraphim. We are under attack!"

Olivia dropped the cup from her hand, breaking it on the ground and spraying hot coffee on her boots. She hardly noticed, however. She became totally alert in an instant, her body stiffening like a coiled spring about to release its force.

Olivia answered, her voice calm and steady although adrenaline coursed through her veins: "This is Coast Guard command. Please state your position and the nature of your emergency."

On the other side, the voice sounded faint but composed. "We're approximately 30 nautical miles off the coast. They came out of nowhere... highly armed... Oh God, they're killing everyone!"

Olivia's brain spun through the options. Pirates? Terrorists? Organized drug cartels? Whatever the perils, she understood that time was of critical importance. Her eyes flaming with determination, she turned to her team. "Sound the alert. We have a situation."

The command center exploded in controlled chaos. Alarms went off, crew members hurried to their positions, and the air buzzed with palpable tension. Jack Tanner, Olivia's second-in-command, appeared by her side amidst the hustle. His tough look mirrored Olivia's own, set in grim resolve.

Jack asked in his calm, steady voice, "What's the situation, Captain?"

Olivia filled him in quickly on the distress call. "The yacht Seraphim is under attack by an unidentified number of highly armed assailants. We've lost contact."

Jack nodded, his mind already developing tactical options. "I'll equip the response team. We'll be ready to move in five."

As Jack rushed to prepare the squad, Olivia grabbed the secure line to call Admiral Marcus Blackwell. Two rings and then the admiral's austere voice responded.

"Blackwell here. What's the situation, Raines?"

Olivia relayed the data quickly and accurately, her years of expertise evident in her concise report. "We lost contact shortly after. Request permission to respond."

On the other end of the line, there was a brief pause. Blackwell's voice weighed heavily with authority as he spoke again. "Permission granted, Captain. But proceed with extreme caution. We don't know what you're walking into. Should this be as bad as it sounds, we could be looking at an international incident."

"Understood, sir. We'll keep you informed and move carefully."

Olivia could feel duty weighing on her as she hung up the phone. Every second mattered because lives were on the line. Her movements were deliberate and forceful as she moved toward the docks.

The Sentinel, a Coast Guard cutter, was poised for action, her sleek design a reassuring sight. As Olivia approached, she could see her staff already in motion, loading equipment and preparing for departure. Jack Tanner stood at the gangway, supervising the last-minute preparations.

Jack reported as Olivia boarded, "We're locked and loaded, Captain. The crew is prepared for anything."

Olivia nodded, gazing broadly over her team. Every face she saw was set with determination, ready to meet whatever challenges lay ahead. Knowing she could rely on every single member of her team filled her with pride.

"Alright, people," Olivia called out over the deck. "We don't know what we're walking into, so stay sharp and watch each other's backs. The luxury yacht Seraphim has sent out a distress call; they are under attack by an unknown number of armed assailants."

She paused and met the eyes of each crew member in turn. "This is what we have trained for. Let's bring these people home safe."

A chorus of affirmatives sounded as the team sprang into action. Olivia took her place on the bridge, her hands steady on the controls. She felt in her bones the heavy rumbling of the Sentinel's engines coming to life. The familiar spike of adrenaline coursed through her as they pulled away from the pier, a mixture of excitement and apprehension accompanying every mission.

The Sentinel's powerful engines drove them towards the coordinates of the distressed vessel, purposefully cutting through the waves. Early dawn light glittered on the ocean spray they passed, a beautiful sight that belied the gravity of their task.

On the bridge, Olivia stared out toward the horizon, her mind running through various scenarios. Beside her, Natalie Harper, the team's communications specialist, monitored the radio channels, her fingers dancing over the equipment in search of any further messages from the Seraphim.

Glancing at Natalie, Olivia asked, "Anything?"

Natalie shook her head, concentration furrowing her brow. "Nothing, Captain. It's been radio silence since that initial distress call."

Olivia's jaw tightened. Lack of communication could indicate many things, none of them positive. She pushed the thought aside, focusing on the task at hand. "Keep monitoring. If they so much as whisper, I want to know about it."

As they approached the coordinates, Olivia ordered reduced speed. The atmosphere on the bridge tensed, everyone acutely aware they were entering potentially hostile waters. Raising her binoculars, Olivia scanned the horizon for any sign of the Seraphim.

At first, there was only the vastness of the sea. Then, as if materializing from the morning mist, the elegant silhouette of a luxury vessel emerged. As Olivia took in the scene, her heart sank.

The Seraphim, meant to represent the height of luxury and relaxation, drifted aimlessly on the sea. Dark streaks that Olivia instinctively knew were blood marred her pristine white hull. There was no movement on the deck—no sign of life.

"My God," Jack murmured beside her, his voice barely audible over the engine's hum.

Olivia lowered her binoculars, her face a mask of grim determination. "Prepare to board," she ordered. "Full tactical gear; we don't know if the assailants are still on board."

As the team prepared, Olivia's mind raced through the possibilities. The lack of visible activity could mean the assailants had already left, or that they were lying in wait, ready to ambush any would-be rescuers. She knew they needed to be prepared for anything.

The Sentinel drew alongside the Seraphim, the contrast between the two vessels stark and disturbing. The yacht, built for elegance and comfort, stood in sharp relief against the Coast Guard cutter, all business, built for speed and utility. At least, that's how it had been before whatever catastrophe had visited it.

Olivia led the boarding party, her senses sharp and her weapon ready. Jack Tanner was right behind her, his steady presence a comfort as they stepped onto the blood-stained deck of the Seraphim.

The eerie silence they encountered was broken only by the soft lapping of waves against the hull and the creak of the vessel as it rocked in the ocean. Olivia motioned for the team to spread out, her eyes constantly scanning for any movement—any sign of a threat.

As they moved deeper into the vessel, the true extent of the carnage became apparent. Bodies lay scattered, their once-pristine clothing now darkened with blood. Broken glass crunched underfoot, and bullet holes scarred the walls. The acrid smell of gunpowder and the metallic scent of blood permeated the air.

Olivia forced herself to remain focused even as her stomach turned at the sight. Every corpse, every bloodstain, every overturned piece of furniture could be a clue. She tried to piece together what had happened here, noting the positions of the bodies and the types of injuries.

Jack's voice, tense with anticipation, came over the radio. "Captain, you need to see this."

Olivia made her way to Jack's location, her footsteps echoing in the unnatural quiet. She found him in what appeared to be the main salon of the yacht, a space meant to epitomize luxury but now a scene of unspeakable horror.

Bodies lay sprawled across plush sofas and expensive Persian rugs. A shattered crystal chandelier lay on the floor, its pieces glittering grotesquely in pools of blood. But it was what Jack was pointing at that drew Olivia's attention.

Written on the far wall, in what could only be blood, was a single word: "JUDGEMENT".

A chill ran down Olivia's spine. This was no ordinary act of piracy or robbery. This was something else entirely—something far more sinister.

"What the hell happened here?" Jack asked, his face pale beneath his tan.

Olivia shook her head, her mind reeling. "I don't know," she said. "But whatever it was, it's bigger than we thought. We need to secure the scene and call for backup."

As if on cue, Natalie's voice crackled over the radio. "Captain, I've established a secure link with Admiral Blackwell. He's requesting an update."

Olivia took a deep breath, steeling herself for the conversation ahead. "Patch him through, Natalie."

Admiral Blackwell's stern voice filled her earpiece. "Report, Captain Raines. What's the situation?"

Olivia spoke steadily as she relayed the grim details of what they had discovered. With each word, she could almost feel the admiral's tension rising.

There was a long silence after she finished before Blackwell spoke again. "This is worse than we feared, Raines. I'm sending additional support your way, including a forensics team. In the meantime, secure the scene. No one goes in or out without my express permission. Is that clear?"

"Crystal clear, sir," Olivia replied.

As she ended the call, Olivia turned to Jack. "You heard the admiral. Let's lock this place down tight."

Over the next few hours, Olivia and her team worked methodically, securing every part of the yacht. Despite the horrific conditions, their training kicked in, and they moved with practiced precision. Jack Tanner set up a perimeter to ensure no one could approach the vessel undetected.

As they worked, Olivia's mind whirled with questions. Who could have done this? And why? The level of brutality suggested something beyond a simple heist gone wrong. The cryptic writing on the wall hinted at some kind of twisted ideology at work.

Natalie Harper appeared on the scene with her equipment. "I'm ready to start the digital sweep, Captain," she said. "If there's any electronic evidence left behind, I'll find it."

Olivia nodded her approval. "Good. Start with the yacht's surveillance system. If we're lucky, we might catch a glimpse of our perpetrators."

As Natalie set to work, Olivia began the grim task of carefully examining the bodies. Each victim told a story: the angle of the wounds, the position of the body, the expression of terror frozen on their features. Forcing herself to look dispassionately, Olivia knew that every detail could be crucial in unraveling this horrific crime.

The victims were a mix of guests and crew, their once-immaculate clothing now stained and torn. Olivia noted that some of the dead lacked defensive wounds, suggesting they had been taken by surprise. The attack must have been swift and merciless.

As she worked, Olivia heard Jack call out from another room. "Captain, I've found something."

She made her way to his location and found him in what appeared to be the captain's quarters. Jack was kneeling next to a barely visible seam in a section of the wall.

"There's a hidden compartment here," he said, pressing lightly on the panel. It clicked softly and swung open to reveal a small space packed with documents and other items.

Olivia's eyebrows rose as she surveyed the contents. The small chamber contained stacks of papers, USB drives, and what looked like multiple passports. "Good work, Jack," she said, her mind immediately racing with the implications of this discovery. "This might be the key to understanding what happened here."

As they carefully removed the items from the compartment, Olivia couldn't shake the feeling that they had stumbled onto something much bigger than a simple yacht massacre. The hidden documents, the cryptic message, the sheer brutality of the attack—all pointed to a complex and potentially far-reaching conspiracy.

"Bag and tag everything," Olivia ordered. "We need to get all of this back to the lab for analysis."

As Jack began securing the evidence, Olivia's radio crackled to life. It was Natalie. "Captain, you need to see this. I've recovered some of the surveillance footage. It's partially corrupted, but..."

Olivia made her way to where Natalie had set up her equipment. The communications specialist turned from her screen, her face pale. "I've never seen anything like this, Captain," she said, her voice shaking.

Olivia leaned in to view the footage. Though the video was grainy and fragmented, what she saw sent a chill down her spine. Dark figures, their faces hidden behind terrifying masks, moved with military precision through the vessel. Their movements suggested extensive training, and they dispatched the yacht's passengers with ruthless efficiency.

But what truly shocked Olivia was what came next. As the last victim fell, one of the assailants turned to face the camera squarely. Even with the graininess of the video, Olivia could make out an insignia on the attacker's uniform—a symbol she recognized with a jolt of alarm.

It was the emblem of an elite military unit, one that officially didn't exist.

Olivia straightened, her mind reeling with the implications. This wasn't just a crime. This was something that could have global ramifications and far beyond their jurisdiction.

"Natalie, secure that footage," Olivia said, her voice taut. "No one sees it without my direct authorization."

Natalie nodded and began encrypting the video file while Olivia stepped away, needing a moment to process what she had witnessed. She made her way to the yacht's deck, hoping the sea air might help clear her head.

The sun now high in the sky, its cheerful rays contrasted sharply with the darkness they had uncovered. Feeling anything but peaceful herself, Olivia gazed out over the calm waves. She knew that what they had unearthed today would set in motion a chain of events capable of shaking the very foundations of national security.

As she stood there organizing her thoughts, Olivia heard footsteps behind her. Jack joined her at the railing, his expression grim.

"What do you make of all this, Captain?" he asked, his voice low.

Olivia shook her head slightly. "I'm not sure, Jack," she said. "But one thing's certain—we're in way over our heads here. This goes beyond anything we've dealt with before."

Jack nodded, his look pensive. "So, what's our next move?"

Olivia turned to face him, resolve setting her jaw. "We do our job," she said firmly. "We file our reports, we secure the evidence, and we prepare for whatever comes next. Because mark my words, Jack—this is just the beginning."

As they stood there, the gentle lapping of waves against the hull seemed to mock the gravity of their situation. Olivia knew that the coming days would test her and her team in ways they had never been tested before. But as she looked at Jack, seeing the same determination in his eyes that she felt in her heart, she knew they were ready for the challenge.

"Let's get back to work," she said, straightening her shoulders. "We've got a long road ahead of us."

Jack nodded, a hint of a smile touching his lips. "Aye, aye, Captain."

As they turned to head back into the yacht's interior, Olivia cast one last glance at the horizon. The sea, once a source of comfort and familiarity, now seemed to harbor untold dangers. But whatever lay ahead, whatever sinister forces they were up against, Olivia was determined to see this through to the end.

The truth was out there, hidden beneath layers of secrecy and deception. And Olivia Raines, seasoned Coast Guard captain turned reluctant detective, was going to find it—no matter the cost.

Chapter 2: The Investigation Begins

The morning sun cast long shadows across the bustling port as Coast Guard Captain Olivia Raines strode toward the imposing headquarters building. Her steps were purposeful, her expression a mask of determination that barely concealed the turmoil beneath. The past twenty-four hours' events weighed heavily on her mind, images of the massacre aboard the Seraphim replaying in vivid, gruesome detail.

As she approached the entrance, Olivia took a deep breath, steeling herself for the meeting ahead. She knew that the next few hours would be crucial in shaping the course of the investigation. The security guard at the desk nodded in recognition as she passed, her reputation preceding her.

The elevator ride to Admiral Marcus Blackwell's office on the top floor seemed interminable. Olivia used the time to gather her thoughts, mentally rehearsing the key points of her report. When the doors finally slid open, she stepped out into a corridor adorned with framed photographs chronicling the Coast Guard's illustrious history. At the end of the hall, a polished brass nameplate marked her destination: "Admiral Marcus Blackwell, Commander of Coast Guard Pacific Area."

Olivia rapped her knuckles against the solid oak door, her knock echoing in the quiet hallway. A gruff "Enter" sounded from within, and she pushed the door open, stepping into the familiar confines of Admiral Blackwell's office.

The room was a testament to Blackwell's long and distinguished career. Model ships adorned every shelf and cabinet, their intricate rigging and polished brass fittings gleaming in the sunlight that streamed through the large windows. Charts and maps covered one wall, dotted with colorful pins marking past and current operations. The smell of old leather and sea salt permeated the air, a comforting reminder of the world they both loved.

Admiral Blackwell stood behind his desk, his silver hair neatly combed, his uniform impeccable as always. His weathered face bore the lines of countless missions and weighty decisions, but his eyes were sharp and alert as they met Olivia's.

"Captain Raines," he said, his voice gravelly but warm. "Take a seat." He gestured to one of the chairs in front of his desk.

Olivia complied, setting her briefcase on her lap. "Thank you for seeing me on such short notice, Admiral."

Blackwell waved off her thanks as he lowered himself into his own chair. "These circumstances certainly qualify as an emergency. Now, tell me everything."

Taking a deep breath, Olivia began her report. She spoke clearly and concisely, years of training allowing her to deliver even the most horrific details with professional detachment. She described the scene aboard the Seraphim in meticulous detail – the bodies strewn across the deck, the signs of struggle, the peculiar lack of certain valuables while others remained untouched.

As she spoke, Blackwell's expression grew increasingly grave. His fingers steepled in front of him, occasionally tapping together as he processed the information. When Olivia reached the part about the potential involvement of an international crime syndicate, his eyes narrowed, a frown deepening the lines around his mouth.

"And you're certain about this connection?" he asked, interrupting for the first time since she'd begun.

Olivia nodded. "At this point, the evidence is circumstantial, but the patterns match what we've seen in other cases attributed to the syndicate. The level of violence, the specific items taken, the way the scene was left... it all fits their M.O."

Blackwell leaned back in his chair, his gaze distant as he considered the implications. "This is bigger than we initially thought, then. If the syndicate is indeed involved, we're looking at potential national security implications."

"Yes, sir," Olivia agreed. "That's why I felt it was imperative to bring this to your attention immediately."

The admiral nodded, his expression hardening with resolve. "You did the right thing, Captain. This situation demands swift and decisive action." He leaned forward, his voice taking on a tone of urgency. "I'm assigning additional resources to your team effective immediately. You'll have whatever you need to pursue this investigation."

Relief washed over Olivia. She had hoped for additional support, but hadn't dared to expect it so quickly. "Thank you, sir. We'll put them to good use."

"See that you do," Blackwell replied. "But there's more. Given the potential scope of this case, we can't handle it alone. I've been in touch with the FBI, and they're sending one of their top agents to assist with the investigation."

Olivia felt a flicker of unease at this news. While she understood the necessity of interagency cooperation, she had always preferred to run her investigations without outside interference. "I see," she said, careful to keep her tone neutral. "And when can we expect this agent to arrive?"

A ghost of a smile played across Blackwell's lips. "She's already here. In fact, I'd like you to meet her now." He pressed a button on his desk phone. "Sandra, could you please send Agent Salazar in?"

Moments later, the office door opened, and a woman entered. Olivia rose to her feet, turning to face the newcomer. Agent Elena Salazar strode into the room with an air of quiet confidence, her dark eyes sweeping the office before settling on Olivia. Her athletic build was evident even beneath her crisp suit. Her black hair was pulled back into a neat bun, accentuating her sharp cheekbones and determined jaw.

"Captain Olivia Raines, meet FBI Agent Elena Salazar," Blackwell said, making the introductions. "Agent Salazar, this is Captain Raines, the lead investigator on the Seraphim case."

The two women shook hands, their grips firm as they sized each other up. Olivia could feel the strength in Elena's grasp, matching it with her own. "Agent Salazar," she said, "welcome aboard."

"Thank you, Captain," Elena replied, her voice carrying a hint of a Spanish accent. "I look forward to working with you on this case."

Blackwell gestured for them both to sit. "Agent Salazar has extensive experience dealing with organized crime, particularly international syndicates. Her expertise will be invaluable in tracking down the perpetrators of this massacre."

Elena nodded, her expression serious. "I've been briefed on the situation, and I agree with your assessment that this bears the hallmarks of syndicate activity. If you don't mind, I'd like to outline my approach to the investigation."

Olivia inclined her head, indicating for Elena to continue. As the FBI agent began speaking, laying out her strategies for tracking financial transactions and identifying key players within the syndicate, Olivia found herself impressed by the agent's thoroughness. However, she couldn't help but feel a twinge of concern as Elena delved into areas that Olivia considered to be under Coast Guard jurisdiction.

"Excuse me, Agent Salazar," Olivia interjected as Elena paused for breath. "While I appreciate your expertise, I think it's important that we clarify the chain of command and jurisdictional boundaries before we proceed further."

Elena's eyebrows rose slightly, a flicker of surprise crossing her face before it settled back into a mask of professionalism. "Of course, Captain. I didn't mean to overstep. Perhaps we could discuss the specifics of our collaboration in more detail?"

Admiral Blackwell cleared his throat, drawing both women's attention. "Ladies, let me be clear. This investigation is of the utmost importance, and it will require seamless cooperation between your agencies. I expect you both to work together, leveraging your respective strengths to bring these criminals to justice. Is that understood?"

"Yes, sir," Olivia and Elena responded in unison, exchanging a glance that was part challenge, part grudging respect.

"Good," Blackwell said. "Now, I suggest you two head down to the conference room and start hammering out the details of your joint operation. Time is of the essence."

As they left the admiral's office, Olivia could feel the weight of responsibility settling on her shoulders. She knew that the success of this investigation would depend not only on her own skills but on her ability to work effectively with Elena Salazar. Despite her initial reservations, she was determined to make it work.

The conference room was a hive of activity when they arrived. Maps and photographs from the Seraphim crime scene covered one wall, while another displayed a complex web of known syndicate connections. In the center of the room, a large table was strewn with reports, forensic analyses, and financial records.

Olivia and Elena took seats across from each other, the tension from their earlier interaction still simmering beneath the surface. For a moment, neither spoke, each waiting for the other to make the first move.

Finally, Olivia broke the silence. "Alright, Agent Salazar. Let's start by outlining our respective areas of expertise and how we can best utilize them in this investigation."

Elena nodded, her posture relaxing slightly. "Agreed. As I mentioned earlier, my background is in tracking organized crime through financial channels. I have access to databases and resources that can help us follow the money trail left by the syndicate."

"That could be invaluable," Olivia acknowledged. "From our end, we have extensive maritime intelligence networks and the ability to monitor shipping lanes and suspicious vessel activity. We also have a team of analysts working on decrypting communication logs from the Seraphim."

As they continued to discuss their capabilities and potential strategies, the initial awkwardness began to dissipate. Both women were consummate professionals, and as they delved deeper into the case, their shared commitment to justice overcame any lingering rivalry.

Their discussion was interrupted by a knock at the door. Natalie Harper, the Coast Guard's brilliant young intelligence analyst, poked her head into the room. "Captain Raines? I have some information you might want to see."

Olivia waved her in. "Come in, Natalie. This is FBI Agent Elena Salazar. She'll be working with us on the case."

Natalie nodded a greeting to Elena before spreading out a series of printouts on the table. "I've been working on decrypting the communication logs from the Seraphim, and I think I've found something significant."

Both Olivia and Elena leaned in, their earlier tension forgotten as they focused on this new lead. Natalie pointed to a series of seemingly random numbers and letters. "These encrypted messages appear repeatedly in the logs, always followed by a specific set of coordinates. I believe they may be referencing some kind of drop-off or meeting point."

Elena's eyes lit up with interest. "Excellent work. Have you been able to pinpoint the location?"

Natalie nodded, pulling out a map. "It's a small, isolated dock about fifty miles up the coast. Satellite imagery shows minimal activity in the area, which could make it an ideal spot for clandestine meetings."

Olivia felt a surge of excitement. This could be the break they needed. "Natalie, I want you to continue working on these logs. See if you can decrypt any more of the messages or identify any patterns in the communication."

"Yes, ma'am," Natalie replied, gathering her materials.

As the young analyst left, Olivia turned to Elena. "I think we should move on this lead immediately. A small, covert team could investigate the dock without alerting the syndicate to our interest."

Elena nodded in agreement. "I concur. We should also set up surveillance on the area in case any of our suspects decide to make an appearance."

For the next hour, they worked together to plan their approach, their earlier misgivings fading as they focused on the task at hand. By the time they finished, a comprehensive strategy had taken shape, combining the strengths of both the Coast Guard and the FBI.

As they prepared to brief the rest of the team, Olivia found herself reassessing her initial impression of Elena. The FBI agent's insights and strategic thinking had proven invaluable, complementing Olivia's own expertise in ways she hadn't anticipated.

The briefing room was packed when they entered, faces both familiar and new turning to watch as Olivia took her place at the front. She could feel the weight of their expectations, the collective desire for answers and justice.

"Thank you all for coming," she began, her voice steady and confident. "As you know, we're dealing with a situation of unprecedented severity. The massacre aboard the Seraphim was not just a random act of violence, but a calculated move by a dangerous international crime syndicate."

A murmur ran through the room at this confirmation. Olivia held up a hand for silence before continuing. "Thanks to the hard work of our intelligence team, we've uncovered a potential lead." She nodded to Natalie, who brought up a series of images on the large screen behind them.

"These decrypted communications point to a possible meeting or drop-off point at an isolated dock north of here. Agent Salazar and I will be leading a team to investigate this location."

Elena stepped forward, adding her own insights to the briefing. She outlined the FBI's role in the investigation, emphasizing the importance of interagency cooperation. As she spoke, Olivia could see the team's initial wariness towards the FBI agent beginning to fade, replaced by respect for her obvious expertise.

When the briefing concluded, the room buzzed with purposeful energy. Team members dispersed to their assigned tasks, the gravity of the situation tempered by a renewed sense of hope.

As the room emptied, Olivia felt a presence at her side. She turned to find Elena standing there, a determined glint in her eye. "Ready to gear up, Captain?" the FBI agent asked.

Olivia nodded, a small smile tugging at the corners of her mouth. "Let's go catch some bad guys, Agent Salazar."

The next hour passed in a flurry of activity as they prepared for the mission. Weapons were checked and double-checked, communication devices tested, and plans reviewed one final time. As they made their way to the helipad, Olivia could feel the familiar mix of adrenaline and focus settling over her.

The helicopter waited on the pad, its rotors already beginning to spin. The pilot gave them a thumbs up as they approached, shouting over the growing roar of the engine. "We're all set, Captain!"

Olivia nodded, then turned to her team. "Remember, this is a recon mission. We go in quiet, gather what intel we can, and get out. No unnecessary risks. Understood?"

A chorus of affirmatives answered her. Satisfied, she climbed aboard, taking her seat next to Elena. As the helicopter lifted off, the coast falling away beneath them, Olivia allowed herself a moment of reflection.

The partnership with Elena, which had started so tensely, now felt like a source of strength. Their differing perspectives and skills, rather than causing conflict, were proving to be complementary. As they flew towards the unknown dangers ahead, Olivia felt a growing certainty that together, they stood a real chance of unraveling this deadly mystery.

The isolated dock came into view as the helicopter approached, a lonely strip of weathered wood jutting out into the choppy waters. From above, it looked innocuous enough, but Olivia knew appearances could be deceiving.

They set down a short distance away, the team disembarking swiftly and silently. Olivia and Elena took point, their weapons at the ready as they advanced on the structure. The wood creaked ominously underfoot, the salt-laden air thick with tension.

At first glance, the dock appeared abandoned, showing no signs of recent activity. But as they moved further along its length, Elena held up a hand, signaling for the team to stop. She knelt, examining something on the worn planks.

"Fresh tire tracks," she murmured, her fingers tracing the faint impressions. "Someone's been here recently."

Olivia nodded, her eyes scanning the surrounding area with renewed intensity. "Fan out," she ordered quietly. "Search every inch of this place."

The team moved with practiced efficiency, leaving no stone unturned. It was Jack Tanner, one of Olivia's most experienced officers, who made the crucial discovery. "Captain!" he called out, his voice tight with excitement. "You're going to want to see this."

Olivia and Elena hurried over to where Jack stood next to a weathered shed at the far end of the dock. As they approached, he pointed to a section of the floor. "The boards here are newer than the rest. I think there might be something underneath."

Working together, they carefully pried up the planks, revealing a hidden compartment beneath. Inside, they found a cache of weapons – high-powered rifles, explosives, and what looked like components for improvised explosive devices. Alongside the weapons were stacks of documents, their pages filled with coded messages and what appeared to be shipping manifests.

As they examined their find, Olivia felt a mix of triumph and dread. This was the break they'd been hoping for, concrete evidence of the syndicate's operations. But the nature and quantity of the weapons spoke to something far more sinister than they had initially suspected.

Elena voiced the thought that was running through both their minds. "This isn't just about drug smuggling or human trafficking. They're planning something big, something that could put countless lives at risk."

Olivia nodded grimly. "We need to get this back to headquarters immediately. Every second counts now."

As they carefully documented and collected the evidence, Olivia couldn't shake the feeling that they had stumbled upon something much larger and more dangerous than they had anticipated. The game had changed, the stakes raised to a level that sent a chill down her spine.

But as she looked around at her team – at Elena, whose determination matched her own, at Jack, whose years of experience were evident in his methodical approach to cataloging the evidence – she felt a surge of pride and determination. They were the best at what they did, and together, they stood a chance of stopping whatever nefarious plot was unfolding.

"Alright, team," Olivia called out, her voice steady and authoritative. "Let's wrap this up and move out. We've got a long night ahead of us."

As they made their way back to the helicopter, the weight of their discovery heavy in their arms and on their minds, Olivia caught Elena's eye. There was a moment of silent communication between them, a shared understanding of the magnitude of what lay ahead.

The chopper blades whirred to life, lifting them away from the isolated dock and back towards civilization. As the coastline receded behind them, Olivia's mind was already racing, piecing together the puzzle, preparing for the battles to come.

This was just the beginning, she knew. But with her team by her side and the unexpected alliance with Elena Salazar, Olivia felt ready to face whatever challenges lay ahead. The syndicate had made their move, and now it was time for Olivia and her team to strike back.

As the lights of the city came into view, Olivia steeled herself for the long night of analysis and planning that awaited them. Whatever the syndicate was planning, she was determined to stop it. The lives of countless innocent people depended on it, and she had no intention of letting them down.

The helicopter touched down on the headquarters' rooftop helipad with a gentle thud. As the rotors slowed, Olivia turned to her team. "Great work out there, everyone. Now comes the hard part. I want all evidence cataloged and secured within the hour. Natalie, get started on those documents immediately. We need to know what's in them."

Elena nodded in agreement. "I'll contact my team at the FBI. We'll need every resource we can get to crack those codes quickly."

As they descended to the main floor, the buzz of activity hit them like a wave. Word of their discovery had already spread, and the office was alive with purpose. Analysts huddled over computer screens, phones rang incessantly, and the air crackled with a mixture of tension and excitement.

Admiral Blackwell met them at the entrance to the situation room, his face grave. "Captain, Agent Salazar, I need a full briefing. Now."

For the next hour, Olivia and Elena took turns outlining their findings, laying out the evidence on the large central table. As they spoke, Blackwell's frown deepened, the lines on his face etched with concern.

"This is worse than we thought," he said finally, running a hand through his silver hair. "If they're stockpiling this kind of firepower, we could be looking at a major terrorist attack."

Olivia nodded, her jaw set with determination. "We won't let that happen, sir. We've got our best people on it, and with the FBI's resources," she glanced at Elena, who gave a slight nod, "we stand a good chance of stopping them before they can act."

"I hope you're right, Captain," Blackwell said, his voice heavy with the weight of command. "Because if we fail, the consequences will be catastrophic."

As they left the situation room, Olivia felt a hand on her arm. She turned to find Elena looking at her, a mixture of respect and concern in her dark eyes.

"You know," Elena said quietly, "when I was assigned to this case, I wasn't sure what to expect. I've worked with other agencies before, and it's not always... smooth."

Olivia couldn't help but smile. "I know the feeling. I wasn't exactly thrilled about the idea of FBI involvement at first."

Elena nodded, a wry smile tugging at her lips. "But after today... I'm glad we're working together on this. You've got a good team, Olivia. And a good leader."

"Thanks," Olivia replied, feeling a warmth of camaraderie she hadn't expected. "Your expertise has already proved invaluable. I have a feeling we're going to need it even more in the days to come."

They shared a moment of understanding before Elena spoke again. "I should check in with my superiors, brief them on what we've found. But after that, what do you say we grab some coffee and start going through those documents?"

Olivia nodded, suppressing a yawn. "Sounds good. I have a feeling it's going to be a long night."

As Elena walked away, Olivia took a moment to survey the bustling office. Her team was hard at work, each person focused on their task with unwavering dedication. She felt a surge of pride mixed with a steely resolve. They had a long way to go, but they'd made a crucial first step.

Turning back to her office, Olivia's mind was already racing, piecing together the puzzle, preparing for the battles to come. The syndicate had made their move, and now it was time for Olivia and her team to strike back. As she reached for the first stack of reports on her desk, she allowed herself a small, determined smile.

The real work was just beginning, but Olivia Raines was ready for the challenge. Whatever the syndicate had planned, she and her team would be there to stop it. The investigation had taken a dramatic turn, and the clock was ticking. But with every passing minute, they were getting closer to the truth.

And Olivia wouldn't rest until they found it.

Chapter 3: Finding Hints

The Coast Guard's briefing room's fluorescent lights buzzed above, harshly illuminating Olivia Raines' and Elena Salazar's faces. They sat in a sea of papers, folders strewn across the table like fallen leaves. As they dug further into the mystery surrounding the luxury boat Seraphim, the air was thick with the scent of coffee and tension.

On the large screen dominating one wall, Natalie Harper's fingers spread over the keyboard, fetching up registration data and ownership records. Olivia leaned closer, focusing her eyes to examine the material.

"There," Elena pointed to a name that stood out among the others. "Viktor Kovalenko. Why does it sound familiar?"

Olivia's mind raced, connecting whispered rumors and dots from previous cases. "Elena, he's an arms dealer. Well-known for his opulent lifestyle and dark connections."

Their knowing gaze reflected the weight of this revelation settling over them like a thick blanket. Turning back to her computer, Elena entered the FBI database, her fingertips dancing over the keys. Moments later, her suspicions were validated.

"Olivia, look at this," she said, her voice tense. "Kovalenko is directly connected to the global crime syndicate run by Andrei Volkov."

A shiver ran down Olivia's spine at the name. Volkov was a ghost—a phantom that had eluded law enforcement for years. His influence spanned continents, leaving a trail of bloodshed and corruption in his wake. And now, somehow, he was linked to the atrocity aboard the Seraphim.

"We need to dig deeper," Olivia remarked, her voice tinged with quiet determination. "This is just the tip of the iceberg."

OLIVIA AND JACK TANNER were back on the blood-stained deck of the Seraphim as the sun climbed higher in the sky, casting long shadows across the lake. The bitter scent of copper still lingered in the air, a grim reminder of the carnage that had unfolded here.

Their footsteps echoed in the eerie silence as they methodically worked their way through the vessel's interior. Every cabin, every nook and cranny was examined painstakingly. Olivia's sharp eye caught minute details: a slight discoloration in the wood paneling, an almost imperceptible seam where none should exist.

"Jack," she said softly, sliding her gloved hand along the cabin wall. "Something's off about this section."

Tanner joined her, his brow furrowed in concentration. With practiced precision, he worked a small tool into the barely visible crack. A soft click produced a panel that swung open, revealing a hidden compartment.

They peered inside, and the air seemed to grow colder. Before them lay row upon row of meticulously arranged assault rifles, grenades, and other instruments of death. This armament, enough to equip a small army, was hidden in plain sight aboard the luxurious boat.

"My God," Jack said, eyes wide. "This is bigger than we imagined."

Olivia nodded grimly, her thoughts already racing ahead to the implications of this discovery. "Jack, tag and bag every item. We need to know exactly what we're dealing with here."

As they worked, cataloging and securing each piece of evidence, Olivia couldn't shake the feeling that they had stumbled upon something far more sinister than a simple boat massacre. She realized that unraveling this conspiracy would be the most challenging case of her career, with tendrils reaching further than she had ever imagined.

BACK AT THE COAST GUARD facility, the forensic lab buzzed with activity. Dr. Lila Shah, the chief medical examiner, laid out the weapons from the Seraphim with practiced precision. Olivia leaned against a nearby counter, watching intently with folded arms.

"What can you tell me, Lila?" she asked, her voice taut with anticipation.

Dr. Shah looked up, her dark eyes serious behind her protective goggles. "Olivia, this is a professional's cache. These aren't run-of-the-mill black market firearms. We're looking at military-grade, top-quality armaments."

As she spoke, Dr. Shah carefully swabbed each weapon, searching for DNA, blood, or other identifying marks. Her movements were precise, each action deliberate and focused.

"There's more," she said, holding up a swab. "Several of these weapons show traces of tissue and blood. They've been used recently, and violently."

Olivia's jaw clenched. "Can you match the blood to our victims from the yacht?"

"I'll run the tests, but given the circumstances, I'd say it's highly likely."

As they discussed various scenarios, Dr. Shah's computer beeped, drawing their attention. "The serial numbers," she murmured, a note of quiet astonishment in her voice. "They match a set of weapons reported stolen from Eastern European military shipments last month."

A chill ran down Olivia's spine. The scope of this operation was expanding by the minute, crossing national borders and reaching into the highest levels of authority. This was no longer just about a yacht massacre; it was about a vast, complex global criminal network.

"Good work, Lila," Olivia said, her thoughts already racing ahead to the next steps. "Keep digging. I have a feeling we've barely scratched the surface here."

As she left the laboratory, Olivia's determination burned brighter than ever. They were onto something big, something that could potentially upend the foundations of global crime. But with that realization came a grim consideration: the higher the stakes, the more dangerous their adversary would become.

THE SITUATION ROOM hummed with tension as Olivia and Elena worked to piece together the bigger picture. Whiteboards covering the walls were filled with names, dates, and connecting lines that resembled an intricate spider's web. At the center of it all, two names stood out: Viktor Kovalenko and Andrei Volkov.

On the main screen, Natalie Harper's fingers flew over the keyboard, pulling up satellite imagery and communication logs. "I've got something," she said, her voice tight with excitement. "There's been a series of encrypted messages between Kovalenko's yacht and several locations in the Caribbean."

Elena leaned forward, her eyes narrowing as she examined the data. "Look at these financial transactions," she said, pointing to a sequence of figures on her screen. "Large amounts flowing through shell companies, all linked back to Kovalenko's accounts. And the timing..."

"Coincides with the communications," Olivia finished, the pieces falling into place. "They're planning something big."

As they delved deeper into the data, a clearer picture began to emerge. The yacht massacre wasn't an isolated incident, but a warning—a brutal message sent to someone who had crossed the syndicate.

"But why?" Elena mused, running a frustrated hand through her hair. "What deal went south? And who were they sending a message to?"

Olivia stepped back, surveying the entire board. Her mind raced, connecting dots and filling in blanks. "We're missing something," she said quietly. "Some piece that ties it all together."

As if on cue, Natalie's computer pinged. "Incoming report from Interpol," she said, quickly scanning the document. "Chatter about a major weapons shipment headed for the Caribbean has been increasing. No specific location yet, but we're talking about military-grade weaponry, enough to arm a small army."

The room fell silent as the implications sank in. This went beyond drugs or money laundering now. The syndicate was deeply involved in arms trafficking, capable of destabilizing entire regions.

Olivia's words cut through the tension. "Alright, listen up. We have a clear objective now. We need to hit this syndicate where it hurts: their money and supply lines. That's how we bring them down. Natalie, I want every bit of intel you can find on that weapons shipment. Elena, dig deeper into those financial records. Follow the money, wherever it leads."

As the team dispersed to carry out their assignments, Olivia felt a mix of excitement and trepidation. They were close, closer than anyone had ever come to bringing down Volkov's empire. But with each step forward, the stakes grew higher. She knew that before this was over, they would be tested in ways they had never imagined.

OLIVIA GATHERED THE team in the conference room, which buzzed with nervous energy. Maps and satellite images covered the table, each marked with potential targets and areas of interest. Every face in the room was etched with determination, aware that the next few hours could change everything.

"Alright, people, listen up," Olivia said, her voice firm and commanding. "We have a unique opportunity here to seriously cripple Volkov's operation. But we need to strike hard and fast."

Elena stepped forward, pointing to a cluster of locations on the main map. "Based on our intelligence, Kovalenko's next major shipment is headed to this Caribbean island. It's remote, largely uninhabited, and perfect for their kind of business."

Jack Tanner leaned forward, his face grim with resolve. "I suggest a coordinated effort with local law enforcement. We hit them fast and hard, catch them in the act of handling the goods. If we time it right, we can take out Kovalenko and a significant chunk of their operations in one sweep."

Olivia nodded, weighing the plan. "It's risky, but it might be our best shot. Elena, I want you coordinating with local police and the FBI. Make sure everyone's on board and we have all the necessary clearances."

"On it," Elena said, already reaching for her phone.

"Jack, you'll lead the tactical team. I want our best people on this; we can't afford any mistakes."

Tanner nodded, a gleam of anticipation in his eyes. "We'll be ready."

"Natalie," Olivia said, turning to the young analyst, "you're our eyes and ears. I need real-time intelligence and communication support throughout the operation. If anything changes, if there's even a hint that they've caught wind of our plan, I need to know immediately."

"Understood," Natalie said, her fingers already flying over her tablet as she set up the necessary systems.

As the team dispersed to prepare, Olivia felt a mix of pride and apprehension. They were the best at what they did, each bringing unique skills and expertise to the table. But they were about to take on one of the most deadly criminal organizations in the world. The stakes couldn't be higher.

She caught Elena's eye across the room, and a silent understanding passed between them. They had trained for this, had dedicated their lives to this. Whatever came next, they would face it together.

THE STEADY THRUM OF the helicopter's rotors filled the air as Olivia and Elena made their final preparations. Below them, the coastline stretched out, a patchwork of brilliant blues and greens that belied the danger that lay ahead.

"Latest intel confirms the shipment's arrival coordinates," Elena shouted over the noise, her eyes never leaving the tablet in her hands. "Local sources have eyes on the ground. They're expecting the delivery within the hour."

Olivia nodded, her mind racing through contingencies and backup plans. She activated her comm device, linking up with the rest of the team spread across several vessels headed for the island.

"This is Raines. All units check in."

A series of affirmatives crackled over the line, each team confirming their readiness. Olivia felt a surge of pride; these were some of the finest agents and officers she had ever worked with, and they were about to risk everything.

"Remember," she added, her voice calm and clear, "our primary objective is to secure that cargo and apprehend key members of Kovalenko's organization. But stay alert; these people are dangerous and won't hesitate to use lethal force. Watch each other's backs out there."

As the helicopter banked to bring the island into better view, Olivia's comm device crackled once more. "Agent Raines, this is

Admiral Blackwell. You are cleared to proceed with the operation. Good hunting."

"Copy that, Admiral. We won't let you down."

Turning to Elena, Olivia saw her own determination mirrored in her partner's eyes. They had come so far, uncovered so much, and now they stood on the precipice of something monumental. If they succeeded here, Volkov's entire network could be dealt a crippling blow.

As the helicopter began its descent, Olivia felt the familiar rush of adrenaline and focus. This was what she lived for: the moment when all the research, all the preparation, all the sleepless nights came to fruition.

"Ready?" she asked Elena, though she already knew the answer.

Elena nodded, a fierce smile flashing across her face. "Born ready. Let's go get these bastards."

The moment the helicopter's skids touched down in a small clearing, Olivia was moving. She could see other teams converging from various directions: Coast Guard boats approaching from the water, local law enforcement securing the perimeter.

As she navigated through the underbrush, her weapon at the ready, Olivia's mind was clear and focused. Every rustling leaf, every snapping twig could be a potential threat. But she pressed on, driven by the knowledge that they were so close to exposing a conspiracy that spanned continents.

Ahead, she could just make out voices and the hum of engines. The shipment was here, and with it, the key to bringing down Volkov's empire. Whatever happened next, Olivia knew that tonight would change everything.

Silently signaling her team, Olivia prepared to emerge from the shadows and into the fight of her life. The truth was within reach, and she was determined to grasp it, no matter the cost.

Chapter 4: Andrei Volkov

The lavish cliffside home gleamed golden in the Mediterranean sun, its white marble façade a stark contrast against the turquoise sky. Andrei Volkov stood on a long balcony overlooking the sea, his steely eyes fixed on the horizon. A gentle breeze, carrying the scent of salt and jasmine, belied the murder and mayhem that followed in Volkov's wake.

As Volkov contemplated the empire he had built, his weathered face remained impassive. His fingers, adorned with a single gaudy gold ring, tapped softly and deliberately on the railing. In the distance, a boat sliced through the waves, a reminder of the recent "mess" that required cleaning up.

Volkov turned away from the scenery and headed inside with a barely audible sigh. With each deliberate step down the great staircase, his footfalls resonated through the huge entryway. The interior of the mansion was a testament to wealth and power; exquisite artwork adorned the walls, exotic carpets cushioned his feet, and crystal chandeliers cast prismatic light across polished marble floors.

A hush fell over the assembled group as Volkov entered the grand conference room. His top lieutenants, men who commanded respect and fear in their own right, stood at attention. Eyes lowered deferentially as Volkov took his place at the head of the long, polished table.

"Gentlemen," Volkov's voice was smooth, cultured, with a hint of his Russian heritage. "Shall we begin?"

The meeting commenced without further preamble. Dimitri Sokolov, Volkov's right-hand man, began reporting on their latest arms acquisitions and money laundering operations. His voice was steady, confident as he outlined the complex web of transactions keeping their empire functional.

"The shipment to the Caribbean is on schedule," Sokolov reported. "Our contacts in the region have secured a remote location for the transfer. Local authorities have been... adequately compensated for their cooperation."

Volkov nodded, his expression inscrutable. "And what of our friend Mr. Kovalenko? Has he resolved the minor... inconvenience on his yacht?"

A tense silence descended upon the room. Boris Ivanov, the lieutenant in charge of overseeing their maritime operations, shifted uncomfortably in his seat. Volkov's piercing gaze fixed on him, cold and expectant.

"Mr. Volkov, sir," Ivanov began, his voice barely steady. "There have been complications. The American Coast Guard—"

"Complications?" Volkov interrupted, his voice sharp. The single word chilled the room. "I prefer simplicity, Boris. Especially when it comes to matters involving authorities."

Ivanov stammered, sweat beading on his brow as he tried to explain. "We're working to contain the situation, sir. Our Coast Guard contacts—"

Volkov silenced Ivanov with a raised hand. The room held its collective breath, waiting to see how their leader would react.

"Dimitri," Volkov said softly, his gaze never leaving Ivanov's face. "Please show Mr. Ivanov out. I believe his services are no longer required."

Two burly men materialized behind Ivanov's chair, their intent clear. As they escorted the now-pale lieutenant from the room, Volkov addressed the remaining group.

"Let this serve as a reminder, gentlemen. Our organization thrives on efficiency, discretion, and absolute loyalty. Anything less is... unacceptable."

The meeting continued, the incident with Ivanov hanging over the proceedings like a dark cloud. Volkov outlined their next major operation: delivering a fresh shipment of high-tech weaponry to buyers in the Caribbean.

"This shipment represents a significant investment," Volkov stated, his voice brooking no possibility of misunderstanding. "Its success is crucial to our expansion in the region. I expect every aspect to be executed flawlessly."

As the meeting drew to a close, Volkov raised one final point. "There's the matter of our... inquisitive friends in the American Coast Guard and FBI. They've been asking too many questions, getting too close to our operations."

A predatory smile played at the corners of Volkov's mouth. "I believe it's time we reminded them of the dangers of poking their noses where they don't belong."

As his lieutenants nodded in grim agreement, Volkov felt a familiar thrill of anticipation. The game was afoot, and he intended to win, regardless of the cost.

THOUSANDS OF MILES away, in a bustling American command center, Coast Guard officers Olivia Raines and Elena Salazar were working late into the night. The room hummed with the low murmur of voices and the steady click-clack of keyboards as they worked tirelessly to connect the dots from the yacht massacre to Andrei Volkov.

Olivia stood before a large screen, her eyes darting between graphs and data points. Fragments of intercepted communications, financial records, and satellite imagery coalesced into a complex tapestry of information. Dominating it all was a grainy image of Andrei Volkov, his icy eyes seeming to mock their efforts.

"There has to be a connection we're missing," Olivia muttered, more to herself than to Elena. "Something that ties Volkov directly to the Seraphim massacre."

Elena, hunched over her computer, looked up. "I might have something," she said, her voice taut with excitement. "Look at this. I've been cross-referencing the names from the yacht's guest list with known Volkov associates."

Olivia moved to Elena's side, peering at the screen. Names and faces flashed by, each accompanied by a web of relationships and transactions.

"This guy," Elena pointed to an unremarkable middle-aged man. "Marcus Reeves. He was on the yacht, listed as a 'business consultant,' but look at his financial records."

With a few clicks, Elena pulled up a series of transactions. "He's been making regular payments to a shell company we've linked to Viktor Kovalenko. The payments match exactly with known weapons shipments."

Olivia's eyes widened as she processed the information. "He was Volkov's man on the inside. Overseeing the deal, maybe?"

"And if something went wrong..." Elena trailed off, the implications hanging heavy in the air.

"It would explain the massacre," Olivia said. "Volkov cleaning house, eliminating any loose ends."

They both knew they needed more, but the pieces were starting to fit. Solid, incontrovertible evidence that would stand up in court and bring down not just Volkov, but his entire network.

"Good work, Elena," Olivia murmured, squeezing her partner's shoulder. "Let's dig deeper into Reeves. I want to know everything – his associates, his movements, every penny that's passed through his accounts."

As Elena set to work, Olivia returned to the main screen. The image of Volkov now seemed to loom larger, a reminder of the formidable enemy they faced. But Olivia felt a glimmer of hope. Sooner or later, Volkov would make a mistake. They were getting closer. And when he did slip up, they would be ready.

OVER THE NEXT FEW DAYS, Olivia and Elena delved deep into the murky world of international finance. Working closely with Peter Lawson, a financial crimes specialist whose expertise proved invaluable in navigating the labyrinth of offshore accounts and shell companies Volkov's organization employed.

"It's like trying to catch smoke," Lawson said, his eyes red-rimmed from hours of staring at screens filled with numbers. "Every time we think we've pinned down a transaction, it splits into a dozen different accounts across as many countries."

Olivia nodded, understanding his frustration. "But there has to be a pattern, no matter how complex the system is."

"You're right," Lawson said, a spark of excitement breaking through his fatigue. "And I think I'm starting to see it."

He pulled up a series of transactions, each seemingly unrelated at first glance. But as he guided them through the data, Lawson revealed a pattern. Large sums of money ultimately funneling back to a single source from a dizzying array of accounts.

"It's actually brilliant," Lawson admitted. "They're using a variation of a technique called 'layering.' The money bounces around so many times that by the time it reaches its final destination, it's almost impossible to trace its origin."

"Almost impossible," Elena said, a smile flickering at her lips. "But not quite."

As they dug deeper, more of the puzzle came together. They uncovered a network of front companies, each playing a small part in concealing Volkov's true activities. But what caught Olivia's eye was a recent transaction involving a large transfer that matched intelligence reports of advanced weapons movement in Eastern Europe.

"This is it," Olivia murmured, her voice tense with anticipation. "This transaction is too large to be anything but the weapons shipment we've been hearing about."

Elena leaned in to examine the data. "The timing fits with our intel about increased Caribbean activity. Volkov's planning something big."

At that moment, Elena's phone buzzed. She answered, listening with growing intensity on her face. She spoke briefly, then turned to Olivia with wide eyes.

"That was my contact in the financial sector," she said. "He's uncovered something about Volkov's money laundering operation. Something major."

Olivia felt a surge of adrenaline. They were close, closer than anyone had ever gotten to unraveling Volkov's empire. But that closeness also brought danger. The higher they climbed, the harder Volkov would fight to protect his interests.

"Alright," Olivia said, her voice ringing with determination. "Let's compile everything we've got. It's time to brief the Admiral and plan our next move."

As they gathered their findings, Olivia couldn't shake the feeling that they were on the cusp of something monumental. The next few days would be crucial, and she knew Volkov wouldn't go down without a fight. But for the first time since this investigation began, she allowed herself to hope. They had a chance to bring down one of the most dangerous criminal enterprises in the world, and she was determined to see it through.

THE BRIEFING ROOM WAS a hive of activity as Olivia and Elena prepared to present their findings to Admiral Marcus Blackwell and key officials from various agencies. The tension in the air was palpable; everyone understood the gravity of what they were about to discuss.

Admiral Blackwell, a commanding man with salt-and-pepper hair and piercing blue eyes, sat at the head of the table. "Alright, Raines," he said, his voice gruff but not unkind. "What have you got for us?"

Olivia stood, her posture straight and confident, belying the weight of the past few sleepless nights. "Sir, we've uncovered evidence linking Andrei Volkov's organization to a major weapons shipment bound for the Caribbean."

She then laid out their discoveries, detailing the intricate network of front companies and financial transactions they had unraveled. Behind her, satellite imagery and financial data flashed across screens, painting a damning picture of Volkov's activities.

"Based on our intelligence," Olivia continued, "we believe the shipment is due to arrive within the next 72 hours. This represents our best chance to strike a significant blow against Volkov's network."

Elena stepped forward to take over the briefing. "We propose a coordinated operation to intercept the shipment and apprehend key figures in Volkov's organization, in conjunction with international law enforcement agencies."

Admiral Blackwell leaned forward, his brow furrowed in concentration. "And you're certain about this intel? Volkov's not a man who makes mistakes easily."

"As certain as we can be, sir," Olivia replied. "We've triple-checked every piece of information. This is solid."

The Admiral nodded slowly, considering their words. The room was silent; the weight of the decision hung heavy in the air.

Finally, Blackwell spoke. "Alright, you have the green light. But I want this operation planned down to the last detail. We can't afford any mistakes, not with a target like Volkov."

A collective sigh of relief echoed through the room. Olivia felt a rush of adrenaline; they were really doing this.

"Thank you, sir," she said. "We won't let you down."

As the meeting broke up, Olivia and Elena stayed behind, already starting to sketch out the details of the operation. The workload ahead was daunting, but the path forward was clear.

"We'll need to coordinate with local law enforcement in the Caribbean," Elena said, jotting down ideas. "And arrange for surveillance of the suspected drop site."

Olivia nodded, her mind racing with plans and contingencies. "I want our best tactical team on this, and we'll need real-time satellite coverage of the entire area."

As they worked, Olivia felt a persistent knot in the pit of her stomach. They were going up against a man who had eluded justice for years – one of the most dangerous individuals on the planet. The risks were enormous, but so were the potential rewards.

"Elena," Olivia said softly, and her partner looked up from her notes. "You know this isn't going to be easy. Volkov's not going to go down without a fight."

Elena's eyes met Olivia's, a fierce determination burning in them. "I know. But that's why we're here, right? To take down the bad guys, no matter how tough they are."

Olivia smiled, feeling her resolve strengthened. Elena was right; this was what they had spent years training for. Whatever challenges lay ahead, they would face them together.

As the sun began to set, casting long shadows across the briefing room, Olivia and Elena threw themselves into their work with renewed vigor. They had a chance to make a real difference, to challenge a criminal empire that had caused untold suffering. And they were determined to make the most of it.

THE NEXT FEW DAYS WERE a whirlwind of activity. Working across time zones, Olivia and her team coordinated with international agencies, briefed tactical teams, and fine-tuned every aspect of their plan. The operation was taking shape, a complex ballet of moving parts all converging on a single goal – intercepting Volkov's weapons shipment and dismantling his network.

On the eve of the mission, Olivia stood on the deck of a Coast Guard cutter, watching the sun sink below the horizon. Before her, the Caribbean stretched out, a vast expanse of deepening blue that held both danger and promise.

Elena joined her at the railing, handing her a steaming cup of coffee. "Hell of a view," she said, her voice tinged with a mix of awe and nervous energy.

Olivia nodded, sipping the strong brew. "Makes you remember what we're fighting for," she said softly. "All those people Volkov's hurt, all the lives he's destroyed. We have a chance to put a stop to that."

They stood in companionable silence for a while, each lost in their own thoughts. Finally, Elena spoke. "You know, when I joined the FBI, I never imagined I'd be here, about to take on an international crime lord."

Olivia laughed. "Life has a way of surprising you. But in all this, I couldn't ask for a better partner."

Elena grinned, bumping Olivia's shoulder with her own. "Right back at you, Raines."

As the last sliver of sun disappeared, Olivia felt a sense of calm settle over her. Tomorrow would bring chaos and danger, but for now, she allowed herself this moment of peace. She knew her team was ready, come what may. They had planned for every contingency, prepared for every scenario.

"Alright," Olivia said, straightening up. "Let's do one last briefing with the team. I want everyone sharp and focused for tomorrow."

As they headed back to the command center, Olivia's mind was clear and focused. The trap was set, the pieces in place. Now it was time to spring it and end Andrei Volkov's reign of terror.

BEFORE DAWN BROKE, Olivia and her team were in position, hidden among the lush vegetation of the small Caribbean island. The air was heavy with humidity and tension as they waited for the signal to move.

Olivia's earpiece crackled to life. "Raines, this is Hawkeye. Two boats approaching the north beach. Heavily armed men on board."

"Copy that, Hawkeye," Olivia said, her voice low and steady. She glanced at Elena, who nodded grimly. "Remember, we wait for visual confirmation of the weapons before we move in. All units stand by."

The minutes ticked by with excruciating slowness. Olivia could feel her heart pounding in her chest, adrenaline coursing through her system. This was what they had been working towards for months.

"Visual confirmation," came the whispered report. "Crates match the description of the weapons shipment. They're offloading now."

Olivia took a deep breath. This was it. "All units, move in. Go, go, go!"

The pre-dawn silence was shattered as Olivia's team burst from their hiding places. Shouts of "FBI!" and "Coast Guard!" mingled with the sudden crack of gunfire.

Olivia and Elena moved as one, years of training and partnership evident in their coordinated movements. They advanced towards the beach, taking cover behind a rocky outcropping.

"On your left!" Olivia shouted, spotting a gunman trying to flank Elena. Her partner spun, her shot finding its mark.

The firefight was intense but brief. Volkov's men, caught off guard by the sudden assault, were quickly overwhelmed. Within minutes, the beach was secured, several of Volkov's operatives were in custody, and the weapons shipment was intact.

As the sun began to rise, painting the sky in pinks and golds, Olivia looked around. Coast Guard and FBI agents were securing the site, cataloging the seized weapons, and processing the detainees.

"We did it," Elena murmured, sounding almost disbelieving as she joined Olivia. "We actually did it."

Olivia nodded, a small smile playing on her lips. "It's a big win, but it's not over yet. Volkov's still out there, and he won't be taking this lying down."

As if on cue, Olivia's satellite phone rang. It was Admiral Blackwell. "Raines," he said, his voice tense. "Good work on the weapons seizure. But we've got a developing situation."

Olivia felt her stomach lurch. "What kind of situation, sir?"

"We've intercepted chatter suggesting Volkov's planning some kind of retaliation. He's not happy about losing that shipment. He's out for blood."

Olivia exchanged a worried glance with Elena. "Any specifics on the threat, sir?"

"Nothing concrete yet," Blackwell said. "But this isn't over by a long shot. You and your team should be on high alert."

As she hung up the phone, Olivia felt the weight of responsibility settling heavily on her shoulders. They had dealt a serious blow to Volkov's organization, but in doing so, they had also painted targets on their backs.

"Elena," she said, her voice tinged with grim determination. "Round up the team. We need to plan our next move."

As they headed back towards the command center, Olivia felt as though this was just the beginning. They had won a battle in the war against Andrei Volkov, but the next round promised to be even more dangerous.

THOUSANDS OF MILES away, in his Mediterranean estate, Andrei Volkov stood at his usual spot on the balcony. His posture was rigid, his face a mask of cold fury as he listened to the report of the Caribbean operation's failure.

"And you're certain?" he said, his voice dangerously quiet. "The entire shipment was seized?"

On the other end of the secure line, the man seemed to swallow audibly. "Yes, Mr. Volkov. The Americans knew exactly where to hit us. It was as if they were waiting for us."

Volkov's grip tightened on his phone, his knuckles white. "I see," he said after a long pause. "Thank you for the information. Your loyalty will be remembered."

As he ended the call, Volkov allowed his carefully calibrated mask to slip for just a moment. Raw anger flashed in his eyes, and with a swift, powerful motion, he hurled his phone across the room. It shattered against the wall, pieces scattering across the marble floor.

Volkov took a deep breath, composing himself. This was a significant setback, but he hadn't built his empire by crumbling at the first sign of adversity. No, this called for a measured, calculated response.

He pressed a button on his desk, and moments later, Dimitri Sokolov entered the room. "Sir?" he inquired, his eyes flicking to the broken phone on the floor.

"Dimitri," Volkov said softly, his voice once again cool and controlled. "I believe it's time we reminded our American friends of the consequences of interfering with our business. They seem to have grown rather too bold."

Sokolov nodded, a cruel smile playing at the corners of his mouth. "What did you have in mind, sir?"

Volkov turned back to face the Mediterranean, his mind already working through possibilities. "I want everything we have on the team that led this operation – names, faces, families – every detail. And then..." he said, his eyes glinting with malice, "then we'll show them what happens when they cross Andrei Volkov."

As Sokolov left to carry out his orders, Volkov allowed himself a small, satisfied smile. The Americans may have won this round, but the game was far from over. And he intended to make sure they understood the true cost of their victory.

Back in the Caribbean, oblivious to the storm brewing across the ocean, Olivia and her team were busy securing the seized weapons and processing the arrested operatives. While Volkov's operation had taken a significant hit, everyone knew the threat was far from over, and the mood was one of cautious celebration.

As the sun climbed higher in the sky, Olivia gathered her core team for a debrief. Huddled around a makeshift command center, Elena, Jack Tanner, and Natalie Harper wore mixed expressions of exhaustion and exhilaration.

"First off, excellent work everyone," Olivia said, genuine pride in her voice. "This operation was a major success, and it's down to each one of you."

Nods and smiles were exchanged, though the weight of their situation wasn't lost on anyone.

"That being said," Olivia continued, her tone growing serious, "we can't afford to let our guard down. Volkov's not the type to take this lying down. We need to be prepared for retaliation."

Elena leaned forward, concentration furrowing her brow. "What's our next move, Olivia? Do we try to leverage these captures for more information on Volkov's operation?"

Olivia nodded. "That's part of it. Tanner, I want you to oversee the interrogations. These men might be low-level, but they could have valuable intel."

Jack Tanner nodded curtly, his face still smeared with camouflage paint. "On it, boss. I'll make them sing."

"Natalie," Olivia turned to the young analyst, "I need you to dive deep into the data we've recovered. Phones, laptops, any devices we've seized. There might be communication logs or financial records that lead us to Volkov's inner circle."

Natalie was already furiously tapping at her tablet. "Consider it done. I'll start data extraction right away."

Turning to her partner, Olivia said, "And Elena, you and I are going to start piecing together the bigger picture. This weapons shipment was just one part of Volkov's operation. We need to figure out what he's planning next."

As the team dispersed to their assignments, Olivia felt a mixture of pride and apprehension. They had accomplished something remarkable today, but she couldn't shake the feeling that they had also stirred up a hornet's nest. Volkov was wounded, but that only made him more dangerous.

She looked out at the sparkling Caribbean waters, so calm and at odds with the threats they faced. One thing Olivia knew for certain: the real fight was just beginning, and the stakes had never been higher.

Chapter 5: Internal Strife

As Captain Olivia Raines stood before her crew, her voice was firm as she provided the most recent update on their ongoing investigation. There was palpable tension in the Coast Guard command center. The meeting hummed with a mixture of excitement and anxiety, every member acutely aware of the significant risks involved in untangling the intricate web of marine crime that had ensnared their territory.

Captain Maxwell Thorne's dramatic entrance cut Olivia's speech short. Several officers flinched when the door banged against the wall. Thorne's eyes blazed with rage, his face a mask of barely restrained fury as he strode purposefully toward Olivia.

"Captain Raines," he bellowed, his voice resonating across the suddenly silent room. "A word. Now."

Olivia's jaw clenched almost imperceptibly, but her voice remained cool as she addressed her staff. "We'll continue this briefing later. Dismissed."

Thorne launched into his diatribe as soon as the room emptied. "Just who do you think you are, Raines?" he spat, bringing them mere inches apart. "You have no right to be trampling over my jurisdiction!"

Olivia stood her ground, meeting Thorne's gaze unflinchingly. "With all due respect, Captain Thorne, this investigation spans multiple jurisdictions. We're all working towards the same goal here."

Thorne's face flushed an even deeper shade of red. "The same goal? That's preposterous. You're nothing but a glory hound, trying to make a name for yourself at my expense!"

Their shouting match attracted the attention of nearby crew members, who observed the altercation with a mixture of curiosity and unease. As accusations flew back and forth, neither captain willing to back down, the air crackled with tension.

Admiral Marcus Blackwell's authoritative voice finally cut through the chaos. "Enough!" he thundered, striding into the room with a sharp, disapproving glance. "Both of you, in my office. Now."

Silence reigned on the walk to Admiral Blackwell's office, the tension between Olivia and Thorne almost palpable. The atmosphere grew even heavier when they sat opposite one another, and Blackwell took his place behind the massive wooden desk.

Blackwell's piercing eyes darted between the two captains. "I expected better from both of you," he said in a quiet, controlled tone. "This kind of public display compromises our entire operation. Now, let's get to the heart of this matter."

Thorne leaned forward, his fingers gripping the chair's arms. "Admiral, Captain Raines has been consistently overstepping her bounds. She's interfering with my investigation, pursuing leads without proper authorization, and undermining my authority at every turn."

Olivia responded, her tone measured but firm. "We're dealing with a time-sensitive case spanning multiple jurisdictions. Every moment we waste arguing over territory is a moment the criminals use to their advantage. With respect, sir, Captain Thorne's inaction on several key leads has forced my hand."

Thorne's lip curled in contempt. "Don't pretend this is about efficiency, Raines. We all know you're just looking to make a splash, to get your name in the papers. Some of us actually try to build a career here, not just chase headlines."

The implication hung in the air, and Olivia's eyes narrowed. "Is that what this is about, Thorne? Your political aspirations?"

A flicker of something—surprise, perhaps, or annoyance at being so easily read—crossed Thorne's face before he schooled his features back into a mask of anger. "My career goals are none of your concern, Raines. What matters is that you're trampling all over proper procedure and chain of command."

Admiral Blackwell silenced them both with a raised hand. "Enough. I don't care about your personal ambitions or your interdepartmental squabbles. What I care about is results. Captain Raines, while I appreciate your initiative, you need to follow proper channels. And Captain Thorne, I expect you to be more responsive to emerging leads, regardless of their source. Is that understood?"

Though the tension between them remained unresolved, both captains nodded.

"Good," Blackwell said. "Now, you two need to find a way to work together on this. Our priority is bringing down this crime syndicate, not massaging egos. Dismissed."

As they exited the office, Olivia and Thorne shared a glance that made it clear their disagreement was far from over. The fragile truce that had been established would be tested in the days to come.

Little did Olivia know that her troubles were only beginning. The next day brought an unexpected visitor to Coast Guard headquarters who would throw her entire world into disarray.

Senator Richard Raines strode through the hallways with the confidence of a man accustomed to wielding authority. His presence drew attention; whispers trailed in his wake as he made his way to Admiral Blackwell's office.

Inside, the atmosphere was charged with a wholly different kind of tension. As Senator Raines shook Blackwell's hand, his smile was all political charm. "Admiral, thank you for seeing me on such short notice."

Blackwell nodded, gesturing for the Senator to take a seat. "Of course, Senator. What can I do for you?"

Raines leaned forward, his expression turning grave. "I'm here to discuss the ongoing investigation into the marine crime syndicate. It's causing quite a stir in Washington, Admiral. There are concerns about the impact on public opinion, not to mention the potential national security implications."

Blackwell furrowed his brow. "I assure you, Senator, we're doing everything in our power to bring this case to a swift conclusion."

"I'm sure you are," Raines said, his voice smooth yet forceful. "But the longer this drags on, the more damage it does to public confidence in our institutions. We need results, Admiral, and we need them soon."

As the conversation progressed, it became increasingly clear that Senator Raines was exerting pressure rather than merely expressing concern. Though his words were carefully chosen, the underlying threat was unmistakable. Ignoring his wishes could have serious repercussions for Blackwell's career.

By the time Senator Raines departed, Admiral Blackwell was visibly troubled. He sank heavily into his chair, the weight of political pressure bearing down on him. Though he had vowed to expedite the investigation, his conscience was wracked by the competing demands of political reality and duty.

Neither man was aware that their conversation had not gone entirely unheard. Olivia Raines stood frozen outside the office, catching snippets of the exchange between her father and her commanding officer. Her mind raced as she retreated to her quarters, a whirlwind of emotions threatening to overwhelm her.

Seated on the edge of her bed, memories of her childhood came flooding back. Her father, always putting his political career ahead of his family, had missed countless dinners and skipped school events, too busy to attend. Olivia had long since come to terms with the fact that her father's ambitions would always take precedence, but this... This was different.

She began to review the evidence they had gathered so far, her perspective shifting as she considered her father's possible involvement. She had missed subtle connections until now, but they were glaringly obvious in retrospect. The timing of certain political maneuvers, the way some leads had inexplicably gone cold, all pointed to a disturbing possibility.

Determination settled over Olivia like a shroud. If her father was indeed part of this criminal network, she would uncover the truth, regardless of the personal cost. However, she would need help, and she knew exactly who to ask.

The following morning, Olivia walked purposefully toward the tech lab. Natalie Harper was hunched over a computer, lines of code reflecting off her glasses.

"Natalie," Olivia said softly, and the other woman swiveled to look up. "I need your help with something off the books."

Natalie raised her eyebrows, then nodded and pushed her chair back from the desk. "What's going on, Olivia?"

In hushed tones, Olivia shared her suspicions about Senator Richard Raines. Natalie listened intently, her expression growing more serious with each word.

When Olivia had finished, Natalie said, "This is big, Olivia. Are you sure you want to go down this road?"

Olivia nodded, her resolve unwavering. "I have to know the truth, Natalie. Can you help me?"

"Of course," Natalie said, turning back to face her computer. "Let's see what we can dig up."

For the next few hours, they worked in near silence, the only sounds the gentle hum of computer equipment and the clicking of keys. Natalie's fingers flew over the keyboard, tracing Senator Raines's digital footprint, navigating through layers of encryption and security measures.

Olivia watched, her heart pounding as information began to populate the screen. Financial transactions, encrypted emails, meeting schedules—all began to paint a picture she had hoped but feared wasn't true.

"Olivia," Natalie said quietly, pointing to a set of decrypted emails. "Look at this. These are messages between your father and known associates of Andrei Volkov."

Olivia leaned closer, her eyes scanning the decoded text. Though the implications were clear, the evidence remained circumstantial. Not enough to act on yet, but certainly enough to warrant further investigation.

"Thank you, Natalie," Olivia murmured, her voice thick with emotion. "I know I'm asking a lot, putting you in this position..."

Natalie shook her head and placed a reassuring hand on Olivia's arm. "We're in this together, Olivia. Whatever it takes to uncover the truth."

As she left the tech lab, Olivia's mind was racing through possibilities. She knew what she had to do next, though it wouldn't be easy. Taking a deep breath, she headed towards Admiral Blackwell's office.

She knocked on the door, steeling herself for what was to come. "Enter," came Blackwell's voice from within.

Olivia stepped inside, closing the door behind her. "Admiral, I need to discuss something of utmost importance with you."

Blackwell turned from his desk, lines of worry etching his face. "What is it, Captain Raines?"

Olivia sat across from him and began to lay out what she and Natalie had uncovered. She watched Blackwell's expression shift from concern to disbelief and then to grim understanding.

"Sir," Olivia began, her voice steady despite the turmoil within her, "I know this is a lot to take in, but I believe we have a duty to pursue this lead, regardless of where it takes us or who it implicates."

Blackwell steepled his fingers in front of him, silent for a long moment. When he finally spoke, his voice carried the weight of the decision before him. "You understand the implications of what you're suggesting, Captain? The political fallout could be catastrophic."

Olivia nodded, her resolve unwavering. "I do, sir. But if we ignore this, we're no better than the criminals we're trying to bring down."

Blackwell stared for what seemed like an eternity before finally nodding. "Very well, Captain Raines. You have my support. But proceed with extreme caution. The waters you're about to navigate are treacherous indeed."

Relief and anxiety warred within Olivia as she left the office. Though she now had Blackwell's backing, the real challenge was yet to come. The road ahead was fraught with danger, both personally and professionally. She was about to investigate her own father, a prominent Senator, for possible connections to a criminal syndicate.

As Olivia Raines strode down the hallway, her posture was straight, but the weight of what lay ahead pressed heavily on her shoulders. She had chosen to follow the truth, wherever it might lead. Her eyes fixed on the horizon as she moved forward with purpose.

Olivia was sailing directly into the heart of the storm, and it was only beginning to gather strength.

Chapter 6: The First Betrayal

Olivia Raines was walking across the Coast Guard installation, the sun just rising above the horizon, spreading long shadows across the landscape. The calm morning was passing. The fresh air smelled faintly of salt from the adjacent ocean. Though Olivia had always been an early riser, it was earlier than most would come for their duties. These peaceful moments before the daily tumult set in comforted her.

She turned to face the main structure and saw movement. Jack Tanner stood in a quiet area of the base, somewhat shadowed by a storage container. Jack, her reliable second-in-command, had been by her side for many missions. Though his presence here was not unexpected, Olivia paused at his demeanor.

Jack was softly talking into his phone, his free hand gesturing in brief, frantic motions. He would look around uncomfortably every few seconds, as if fearing being overheard. Years of law enforcement had sharpened Olivia's instincts, which were instantly alert. This was not the Jack she knew—confident, calm, always ready with a sardonic grin and a deft joke.

She approached softly, not wanting to startle him. Jack's comments became clearer as she got closer, albeit still quite evasively ambiguous.

His voice low and anxious, he said, "Can't keep this up much longer." "They're starting to seem dubious. We have to—"

He stopped sharply when he saw Olivia. His manner altered in a flash. His shoulders relaxed, and he started to grin, if a bit forced.

Saying into the phone, "I have to go," he cut off the conversation without waiting for a reply.

Jack greeted Olivia, his voice laid-back. "You're here early."

Olivia watched him for a moment and noticed the slight sheen of perspiration on his forehead despite the chilly morning air. Keeping her voice casual, she said, "Everything alright, Jack?"

"Yeah, of course," he said, perhaps too quickly. "Just some personal stuff. Nothing to worry about."

Olivia nodded, not pressing further even though her mind rang with warning bells. "Okay. We have a busy day ahead. Let's grab some coffee and review the most recent intelligence."

Olivia sensed something was amiss as they headed toward the building. Jack had always been an open book to her, his thoughts and feelings as clear as day. Now, however, it seemed as if a curtain had been drawn over the man she knew so well.

Olivia watched Jack more attentively throughout the day. She noticed how he would seclude himself for unexplained phone calls, the quiet conversations cut short when others walked in. It was subtle, the kind of behavior that those who knew him less well might overlook. For Olivia, however, it resembled a flickering neon sign.

Late in the afternoon came the last straw. Olivia heard Jack's voice wafting from an empty conference room as she was heading back from a meeting with the base commander. Her hand on the doorknob, she paused to listen to his words.

Jack was pleading, "Need more time," his voice barely above a whisper. "Raines is getting close. If we don't act soon, everything we have worked for will be lost."

Olivia's blood ran cold. Her mind whirled with possibilities, each more unsettling than the last. Was Jack being undermined? Had he been turned by Volkov's organization? Or was there something even more ominous afoot?

She forced herself to walk away, her steady, quiet stride belying the turmoil in her mind. She couldn't confront Jack now, not without more information. One thing, however, was clear: the man she had trusted with her life was hiding something, and she was determined to uncover what it was.

A new complication arose at the Coast Guard headquarters as Olivia retreated to her office, attempting to sort out the ramifications of Jack's apparent betrayal. Striding through the front doors with the confidence of a man who feared nothing, Diego Ortega—a name that had surfaced in several intelligence reports—had always been frustratingly elusive.

Olivia observed Diego calmly and assuredly as he talked to the receptionist through the glass walls of her office. He looked immaculate in a custom suit that suggested money and power. His black hair was well-groomed, and his smile, when he flashed it at the young woman seated at the counter, was dazzling.

A moment later, Olivia's phone chimed. "Commander," the voice of the receptionist emerged, somewhat strained. "There's a Diego Ortega here to see you; he says it's urgent."

Olivia steeled herself with a deep breath. "Send him to Interrogation Room 2," she said. "I'll be there in a minute."

Olivia's mind raced with questions as she headed toward the interrogation room. A known quantity in the criminal underworld, Diego Ortega was a Colombian businessman connected to many illegal enterprises. What could he want with the Coast Guard? And why now, as they were closing in on Andrei Volkov?

She entered the room and saw Diego sitting at the table, looking for all the world like he was about to have a business meeting rather than be questioned by law enforcement. As she arrived, he stood with an extended hand and a polite smile.

"Commander Raines," he said, his accent giving his words a melodic lilt. "It's good to finally meet you. Your reputation precedes you."

Olivia shook his hand briefly and settled across from him. "Mr. Ortega," she replied, her voice businesslike. "To what do we owe the pleasure of your visit?"

Diego's smile widened, but Olivia caught a calculating look in his eyes. "I have information," he murmured softly. "Information about Andrei Volkov that you should find most interesting."

Olivia leaned back in her chair, her expression neutral. "And why would you want to provide this information to us?"

"Let's just say that Volkov and I have had a... falling out," Diego said, a sliver of steel tinging his voice. "I believe seeing him removed benefits both of us."

Over the next hour, Diego meticulously detailed Volkov's operations, including information on a sizable weapons shipment scheduled for the coming weeks. The level of detail was astounding if accurate; if genuine, it could be the breakthrough they had been waiting for.

Olivia remained wary, nevertheless. She had been in this business long enough to know that freely provided information often came with unstated costs. As Mr. Ortega concluded his presentation, she asked, "And what do you want in return for this information?"

Diego's expression became solemn. "Protection," he stated simply. "For my family and me. And... perhaps some consideration for my own activities, should they come to light during your investigation."

Olivia nodded slowly. It was roughly what she had anticipated. "Before we can discuss any kind of deal," she replied, "I'll need to verify your information."

Diego nodded quickly. "Of course," he said. "I wouldn't expect anything less."

As Diego was being escorted off the premises, Olivia's mind was racing with the implications of this new information. If Diego's intel proved accurate, it could be the key to dismantling Volkov's entire operation. But relying on a known criminal carried its own risks.

She needed to consult her team. In a secure briefing room, Olivia gathered Elena Salazar and Natalie Harper, presenting Diego's proposition and the information he had provided.

Elena raised the first objections. She stated forcefully, her dark eyes sparkling with intensity, "We can't trust him. Ortega's been involved in everything from drug trafficking to money laundering. Who's to say this isn't some elaborate trap set by Volkov?"

Always the researcher, Natalie pulled up a file on her iPad. "Diego Ortega," she said, her voice cool and measured. "Colombian national, age 42. Known associates include several high-ranking members of various cartels, as well as legitimate businessmen and politicians. He's been on our radar for years, but we've never been able to pin anything specific on him."

She paused and scrolled through the data. "There are some connections to Volkov's organization, mostly through intermediaries. Nothing direct, but enough to suggest that Ortega's claim of inside knowledge could be credible."

Olivia carefully considered every piece of information. She responded at last, "The weapons shipment he mentioned... if we could confirm that, it would go a long way toward establishing his credibility."

Elena nodded grudgingly. "It's a risk," she admitted. "But if Ortega's telling the truth, this could be the break we've been waiting for."

"We proceed with caution," Olivia said. "We'll verify the information about the weapons shipment; if it checks out, we'll consider moving forward with Ortega. But we keep our guard up at all times; this could still be an elaborate setup."

As the meeting concluded, Olivia's thoughts returned to Jack. His behavior, combined with this new development involving Diego Ortega, was weaving a web of complexity that threatened to ensnare their entire investigation. She needed answers, and she needed them soon.

The next three days were a flurry of activity as Olivia's team worked to verify Diego's information. Despite her growing reservations, Jack Tanner was assigned to oversee the surveillance effort. She kept a close eye on him, looking for any sign he might be compromising the mission, but his work was flawless as always.

Using a combination of drones, undercover operatives, and traditional stakeouts, they confirmed the existence of a hidden weapons cache exactly where Diego had indicated. The discovery sent waves of excitement through the team. It was the first solid lead to Volkov's operation they'd had in months.

Olivia personally reviewed the surveillance footage, her eyes keen for any detail they might have missed. The weapons were there, just as Diego had reported: high-grade military hardware not meant for civilian ownership. It was a treasure trove of evidence that lent significant weight to Diego's claims.

Armed with this information, Olivia decided it was time to meet with Diego again. She arranged a neutral, secure location: a small, nondescript office building on the outskirts of town. Elena accompanied her to provide an additional perspective on Diego's behavior and claims, as well as backup.

Diego arrived precisely on time, looking as polished and confident as he had during their previous encounter. He showed no sign of being nervous about meeting with law enforcement.

As they sat down, he began, "I trust you've had time to verify my information," a knowing smirk playing at the corners of his lips.

Olivia nodded, her face impassive. "We have," she agreed. "And now we need to discuss exactly what you know and what you want in return."

Over the next two hours, Diego meticulously laid out Volkov's operations. He detailed shipping routes, front companies, corrupt officials, and intricate money laundering schemes. The depth of information was staggering, and Olivia began to believe Diego might indeed be as well-informed as he claimed.

She remained cautious, however. During a lull in his explanation, she asked, "Why are you really doing this, Mr. Ortega? What's your endgame here?"

Diego's smile faded, replaced by a grim determination. "Volkov is a rabid dog," he said, his voice low and intense. "He's unpredictable, violent. He's upsetting the balance of power in ways that are bad for everyone – including those of us who operate in, let's say, gray areas of the law."

Leaning forward, he locked eyes with Olivia. "I'm a businessman, Commander. I deal in calculated risks and mutual benefits. Volkov? He's a force of chaos. He needs to be put down, for all our sakes."

Olivia considered his words carefully. She believed there was truth in them, but also deliberate omissions. Diego Ortega was playing a dangerous game, and she needed to ensure they weren't merely pawns in his personal vendetta against Volkov.

"If we do this," she said at last, "you understand that you'll be expected to testify? Your involvement will become a matter of public record."

Diego nodded solemnly. "I understand the risks," he replied. "That's why I need guarantees. Protection for my family and myself. And... leniency, should certain aspects of my business come to light during your investigation."

What followed was a delicate negotiation, with both parties carefully weighing every word and promise. Finally, they reached a tentative agreement. Diego would provide full cooperation, including testimony if necessary. In exchange, he and his family would be placed in protective custody, and should any of his illegal activities be uncovered, the Coast Guard would advocate for reduced penalties.

As Diego departed, Olivia felt a mix of hope and trepidation. They had potentially gained a powerful ally in their fight against Volkov, but at what cost? And could a man like Diego Ortega truly be trusted to keep his word?

These questions plagued Olivia as she returned to the Coast Guard base. However, she could no longer ignore another pressing concern. It was time to confront Jack Tanner.

She found him in his office, poring over surveillance logs from their latest operation. He glanced up as she entered, a smile beginning to form on his face before he caught sight of her serious expression.

"Olivia?" he asked, concern evident in his voice. "Is everything okay?"

Closing the door behind her, Olivia said, "We need to talk, Jack. In private."

Jack frowned but nodded, following Olivia to a small, secure conference room. As they sat down, Olivia could sense the tension in his shoulders; his eyes briefly flicked to the door, as if considering an escape route.

"What's going on, Jack?" Olivia asked, her voice firm but not unkind. "And don't tell me it's nothing. I've seen the phone calls, the hushed conversations. You're hiding something, and I need to know what it is."

For a moment, Jack looked as if he might deny it again. But then his shoulders slumped, and he let out a weary sigh. "I was hoping to protect you from this," he said softly.

"Protect me?" Olivia echoed, clearly bewildered. "From what, Jack?"

Jack ran a hand through his hair, a gesture of frustration she had seen many times before. Finally, he spoke. "I have a contact," he admitted. "Someone inside Volkov's organization. They've been feeding me information, trying to help us take him down."

Olivia felt as if all the air had been sucked out of the room. Of all the possibilities she had imagined, this had not been one. "Why didn't you tell me?" she whispered, her voice barely audible.

"Because it's dangerous," Jack replied, his eyes meeting hers with an intensity that surprised her. "My contact... they're taking an enormous risk. The fewer people who know about them, the safer they are. And the safer you are, Olivia. If Volkov ever found out..."

He trailed off, but Olivia could fill in the blanks. If Volkov discovered a mole in his organization, the retribution would be swift and severe. And if he traced that mole back to the Coast Guard's investigation, back to her...

After a long moment of silence, Olivia spoke. "I understand why you did it," she said. "But Jack, we're partners. We're a team. You can't keep something like this from me, no matter how good your intentions are."

Jack nodded, looking thoroughly chastened. "I know," he replied quietly. "I wanted to protect you, Olivia. To give you deniability if things went south."

Olivia leaned across the table, placing her hand on Jack's arm. "I appreciate that," she said. "But from now on, we do this together. Full transparency. Agreed?"

Jack nodded, a small smile finally breaking through his somber demeanor.

As they exited the conference room, Olivia experienced a whirlwind of emotions. Relief that Jack wasn't betraying them, frustration at being kept in the dark, and a renewed determination to see this investigation through to its conclusion.

Yet underlying everything was a new uncertainty. Jack's hidden contact, Diego Ortega's questionable allegiance, the looming threat of Volkov's operation—all these elements combined to create a web of complexity threatening to ensnare them all.

As she watched Jack return to his office, Olivia felt as if this was just the beginning. The first betrayal had been revealed, but she feared it wouldn't be the last. Trust was a precious commodity in the shadowy world they were navigating; she would need to guard it carefully in the days to come.

A new phase in the investigation of Andrei Volkov's activities was unfolding, fraught with risk and uncertainty. But as Olivia gazed out over the bustling Coast Guard facility, she felt a surge of resolve. They had new allies, new information, and a new sense of purpose.

The pieces were falling into place, but the game was far from over. Olivia knew that the real challenge lay ahead. With Jack's inside source, Diego's information, and her team's expertise, they had a fighting chance to bring down Volkov's empire. But the cost of failure would be high, and the path forward was treacherous.

As the sun began to set, casting long shadows across the base, Olivia steeled herself for the battles to come. Whatever lay ahead, she was determined to see it through. The first betrayal had been unveiled, but in this world of shadows and secrets, she knew it was unlikely to be the last.

Chapter 7: Port of Shadows

As the Coast Guard cutter Sentinel glided into the harbor, the Caribbean sun hung low on the horizon, casting long shadows over the picturesque port. Olivia Raines, taking the lead, felt a mixture of excitement and anxiety course through her. This tropical paradise was a far cry from the dangerous undercurrents tugging at its shores, concealing Andrei Volkov's sinister activities behind a facade of sun-drenched tranquility.

Olivia's sharp eyes scanned the bustling wharf as the Sentinel moored. To the casual observer, the scene appeared to be one of vibrant local life and carefree visitors, but Olivia knew better. Within this tapestry of color and movement lurked the threads of a criminal empire threatening to unravel the very fabric of global security.

Elena Salazar's voice cut through Olivia's thoughts. "Ready?" Standing beside her, the FBI agent maintained a relaxed posture, but her eyes were keen, constantly surveying their surroundings.

Olivia nodded, jaw set with determination. "Let's move."

The rest of the crew fell into step behind them as they disembarked. Jack Tanner stayed close to Olivia and Elena, his weathered face a mask of concentration. Their computer specialist, Natalie Harper, clutched a secure laptop case to her chest, her fingers itching to set up their makeshift command center.

The team flowed through the crush of tourists and locals with practiced ease. Olivia marveled at the contradiction of their environment. On one side, pristine beaches and luxurious hotels beckoned to visitors seeking respite. On the other, dilapidated buildings and shadowy alleyways hinted at a world far removed from the glossy travel brochures.

They made their way to an inconspicuous building with rusting shutters and peeling paint—ideal for their operations overlooking the port. Inside, Natalie wasted no time configuring their command center, her fingers flying across keyboards to establish secure lines back to Coast Guard headquarters.

Jack cleared his throat to capture everyone's attention. "Alright, team. Here's what we know." He spread out a map of the port, indicating several red-marked locations. "These are the known hotspots for Volkov's operations. We have warehouses here and here, suspected drop points along this stretch of beach, and a few local businesses we believe are fronts for money laundering."

Olivia leaned in, studying the map intently. "We need to cover as much ground as possible without raising suspicion. Jack, take Rodriguez and Chen. Focus on the warehouse district. Elena and I will hit the local market—it's a good place to gather intel without drawing attention."

As the team dispersed, Olivia felt a familiar thrill of anticipation. This was the calm before the storm, the meticulous dance of preparation that preceded every major operation. She glanced at Elena and saw the same mix of energy and focus mirrored there.

The local market assaulted their senses the moment they entered, a vibrant explosion of color and sound. Bright textiles fluttered in the warm breeze, competing with the enticing aromas of spices and freshly prepared foods. Vendors hawked their wares in a cacophony of languages, creating a linguistic tapestry as varied as the goods on display.

With practiced nonchalance, Olivia and Elena drifted through the crowd, their ears and eyes alert for the slightest hint of suspicious activity. They paused at various stalls, examining handicrafts and sampling local cuisine, all the while probing seemingly innocent questions for information.

"Business good?" Olivia asked a weary fishmonger, eyeing a glistening red snapper.

The old man shrugged, his sun-leathered face creasing into a frown. "Not like it used to be. Too many big ships coming in at night, scaring away the fish."

Olivia and Elena exchanged a glance. Night shipments could be a promising lead.

As they delved deeper into the market, Elena stiffened beside her. She subtly directed Olivia's attention to a quiet corner where two men were engaged in a discreet conversation. One, a local fisherman with a weather-beaten face and calloused hands, was passing a small package to a well-dressed man Olivia recognized from their intelligence briefings—a known associate of Volkov.

Elena casually raised her hand to adjust her hair, using the motion to take a covert photo with a hidden camera. Meanwhile, Olivia kept the pair in her peripheral vision while guiding them to a nearby stall, pretending to examine a selection of colorful scarves.

The exchange ended quickly, both men melting back into the crowd as if nothing had happened. Just as Olivia was about to suggest they tail the Volkov associate, a voice behind them made her pause.

"Beautiful day for shopping, no?"

Turning, they found themselves face-to-face with an elderly woman smiling at them from behind a display of intricately woven baskets. Olivia's instincts prickled at the knowing glint in her eye.

"Indeed it is," Elena replied smoothly. "We're new in town, just taking in the sights."

The old woman's smile widened. "Ah, but some sights are not meant for tourist eyes, yes? Like the big warehouse on the edge of town. Strange noises at night, many trucks coming and going. Not good for sleeping, I tell you."

Olivia felt her pulse quicken. This could be their needed break. "That sounds troublesome. Where exactly is this warehouse? Perhaps we should avoid that area."

The vendor leaned in close, her voice dropping to a conspiratorial whisper. "On the north side, past the old lighthouse. But be careful, beautiful ladies. Some places are not safe for curious eyes."

Olivia and Elena turned away, their minds racing with the implications of this new information, a grateful nod and a small purchased basket serving as cover.

"Jack," Olivia murmured into her concealed comm device, "We have a lead on a warehouse on the north side of town, past the old lighthouse. Heavy nighttime activity."

"Copy that," Jack replied tersely. "We'll recon from a distance; meet you back at base in one hour."

As the sun dipped below the horizon, painting the sky in brilliant hues of orange and pink, Olivia and her team reconvened at their makeshift headquarters. The atmosphere was charged with a mix of nervous tension and anticipation as they prepared for their nighttime operation.

Natalie's fingers flew across the keyboard, pulling up satellite imagery of the suspect warehouse. "It's heavily guarded," she said, zooming in on the perimeter. "Multiple sentries, state-of-the-art security systems. Whatever's in there, Volkov really doesn't want anyone finding out about it."

Jack leaned over her shoulder, his brow furrowed in concentration. "Looks like our best approach is from the southeast. Their camera coverage shows a blind spot there."

Olivia nodded, her mind already formulating a strategy. "Alright, here's how we play it. Elena and I will go in first, nice and quiet. Jack, I want you and your team providing overwatch from these buildings here and here. Natalie, you're our eyes and ears. Any change in guard patterns, any unexpected visitors, I want to know about it immediately."

As the team geared up, checking weapons and communications, Olivia felt a familiar tightening in her chest. This was the point of no return, the moment of truth. Everything they had worked for, all the risks they had taken, it all came down to what they discovered in that warehouse.

Under the cover of darkness, Olivia and Elena approached their target. The warehouse loomed before them, a hulking shadow against the star-studded sky. As they drew closer, Olivia could make out the precise, alert movements of armed guards patrolling the perimeter.

"Two guards approaching your position," Natalie's voice crackled in their earpieces. "ETA 30 seconds."

Barely daring to breathe, Olivia and Elena pressed themselves against the rough concrete wall as the guards passed mere feet from their position. Once the coast was clear, they moved swiftly to the blind spot Jack had identified.

Elena produced a small device from her pack, attaching it to the electronic lock of a side door. Seconds later, a soft click followed, and the door eased open. They slipped inside, immediately enveloped by the warehouse's cavernous gloom.

Night-vision goggles allowed their eyes to adjust, revealing the true scope of Volkov's operation. Row upon row of crates stretched into the darkness, many bearing military insignias that sent a chill down Olivia's spine. This wasn't just a small-time smuggling operation; this was an arsenal.

"My God," Elena breathed, her voice barely audible. "There's enough firepower here to start a war."

Olivia nodded grimly, her mind racing. They needed to document everything, gather as much intelligence as they could before—

A loud clang froze them in place. Footsteps, multiple sets, running swiftly from the far end of the warehouse.

"We've been found," Olivia hissed into her comm. "Jack, be ready for extraction. Natalie, find us another way out of here!"

Olivia and Elena dove for cover behind a stack of crates as the air erupted in a storm of gunfire, bullets ricocheting off metal and concrete. The acrid smell of cordite filled the air, mingling with the dust kicked up by their frantic movements.

"Exit to your left, 50 meters!" Natalie shouted over the chaos. "I've triggered the fire alarm system to create a diversion!"

On cue, sprinklers burst to life overhead, and sirens began to wail. Olivia and Elena took advantage of the confusion, weaving between crates as bullets whizzed past.

They burst out into the crisp night air, only to find their path blocked by more of Volkov's men. For a heart-stopping moment, Olivia thought they were trapped, but suddenly smoke grenades exploded around them, obscuring their position.

"We've got you covered," Jack's voice barked over the comm.

Olivia and Elena ran through the mayhem of gunfire, smoke, and shouting. Their lungs burned, their muscles screamed in protest, but they didn't stop until they were safely ensconced in their getaway vehicle, speeding away from the scene.

As the adrenaline began to ebb, Olivia allowed herself to relax, feeling the dull ache of exertion and the sting of minor wounds. More importantly, they had acquired crucial intelligence about Volkov's operation. They had survived.

Back at their safe house, the team immediately began analyzing the gathered data. Natalie's fingers flew over the keyboard, uploading photos and decrypting messages they had intercepted.

"This is big," she said, her eyes wide as she scanned the information scrolling across her screen. "We're not just looking at weapons smuggling; there are blueprints here for military installations, classified documents... Volkov's planning something massive."

Olivia leaned closer, her brow furrowed as she examined the data. "We need to figure out his endgame. These shipments, the intelligence he's gathered – it all points to a coordinated attack, but where? And when?"

As the team worked through the night, piecing together Volkov's plan, Olivia felt the weight of responsibility settle squarely on her shoulders. The stakes had never been higher, but they were close, tantalizingly close to cracking this conspiracy wide open.

In the early hours of the morning, Olivia found herself on the balcony of their rented office, seeking a moment of solitude to gather her thoughts as the first light of dawn began to creep over the coastline. The night's events played on a loop in her mind, each detail scrutinized for possible leads or missed clues.

She was so deep in thought that she didn't notice Elena's approach until the FBI agent was standing beside her, offering a steaming cup of coffee.

"Thought you could use this," Elena said softly, leaning against the railing.

Olivia accepted the cup gratefully, inhaling the aroma. "Thanks. How are you holding up?"

Elena shrugged, a wry smile flashing across her lips. "Oh, you know. Near-death experiences, international conspiracies – just another day at the office."

Despite the gravity of their situation, Olivia found herself laughing. It was a welcome release of tension, a reminder of their shared humanity in the face of overwhelming circumstances.

As they stood in companionable silence, watching the sun paint the sky in brilliant hues, Olivia felt compelled to share something of herself with her newfound partner.

"You know," she said, her voice low and reflective, "nights like last night... they bring back memories. Not all of them good."

Elena glanced at her, concern and curiosity mingling on her face. "From your Coast Guard days?"

Olivia nodded, her gaze distant. She paused, sipping her coffee to steady herself, then continued, "There was a mission, years ago. A human trafficking ring operating out of Central America. We thought we had it all figured out, had all our bases covered. But we underestimated them, got sloppy." She swallowed hard. "We lost good people that day. And some of the ones we were trying to save... they didn't make it either."

The weight of the memory hung heavily between them. After a moment, Elena responded, her voice gentle but filled with resolve. "That's why you push so hard, isn't it? Why you're willing to take the risks?"

Olivia turned to Elena, her eyes sharp with determination. "Every life we save, every criminal we bring down – it matters. It has to matter. I won't let what happened then happen again. Not if I can help it."

Elena nodded, understanding dawning in her eyes. "I get it. More than you know." She took a deep breath, as if steeling herself for a confession of her own. "My parents... they left everything behind to give me a better life. But the system, the prejudices they faced – it wasn't the American dream they'd hoped for."

She paused, her fingers tightening around her coffee cup. "That's why I joined the FBI. I wanted to make a difference. To protect people who couldn't protect themselves, to fight the corruption that preys on the vulnerable. This case, going after Volkov – it's not just about national security for me. It's personal."

As the sun finally crested the horizon, bathing them in golden light, Olivia felt a new sense of kinship and respect for Elena. They were more alike than she'd initially thought, both driven by personal experiences and a deep-seated desire to right the wrongs they'd witnessed.

"We're going to stop him," Olivia said softly, her voice filled with quiet conviction. "Volkov, his entire network – we're going to bring it all down."

Elena met her gaze, a fierce determination shining in her eyes. "Damn right, we are."

As they turned back to face the awakening city below, Olivia felt her resolve strengthened. The path ahead was treacherous, the odds stacked against them. But standing shoulder to shoulder with Elena, she realized they had a fighting chance.

Whatever Volkov had planned, whatever dark scheme they had yet to uncover, Olivia and her team would be ready. United by their shared commitment to justice and their unwavering determination to see the mission through, they would face it head-on.

The sun climbed higher, burning away the last traces of darkness. A new day had dawned, bringing with it both opportunities and challenges. As Olivia and Elena rejoined their team, eager to dive back into the fray, one thing was clear: the hunt for Andrei Volkov was far from over. But with each step they took, each puzzle piece they uncovered, they drew closer to their goal.

The Caribbean port, with its deceptive beauty and lurking dangers, had proven to be just the beginning. What lay ahead would test them in ways they couldn't yet imagine. But as Olivia looked around at her team—at Jack's unwavering focus, Natalie's sharp intellect, and Elena's steadfast loyalty—she knew they were ready for whatever came next.

The game was afoot, and Olivia Raines was playing to win.

Chapter 8: The Intel Breakthrough

As Natalie Harper leaned over her keyboard, her fingers speeding over the keys with practiced accuracy, the gentle illumination of several computer displays lit her determined face. The Coast Guard intelligence analyst had lost sense of time; the hours merged in a blur of encrypted files and data streams. Long after the rest of the staff had left, Natalie was alone with the faint hum of electronics and the occasional ping of arriving data.

She blinked hard, attempting to concentrate her weary eyes on the never-ending lines of code slinking over her primary screen. Something seemed amiss. She had seen a trend in the decrypted yacht records, a subtle aberration that persisted at the margins of her awareness. Natalie knew long ago to follow her instincts, and right now they were screaming she was on the brink of something significant.

"Come on," she murmured, leaning closer to the screen. "Show me what you're hiding."

Her fingers danced across the keyboard, completing a set of complex instructions. Suddenly, a new window appeared on her screen, revealing a hidden folder buried deep within the yacht's digital records. As Natalie clicked through the files, her heart began to race, and her eyes widened with each new revelation.

"This can't be real," she whispered, her hand automatically reaching for her phone.

But the evidence before her was undeniable: comprehensive plans, letters, and schedules pointing to an imminent terrorist strike on American soil. And at its core, a name that had become all too familiar: Andrei Volkov.

Natalie dialed Olivia Raines, her fingers trembling slightly. The phone rang twice before a sleep-roughened voice answered.

"Raines."

"Olivia, you need to see this. It's Natalie."

Twenty minutes later, Olivia Raines and Elena Salazar burst into the command center, their faces etched with concern. Natalie swiveled in her chair to face them, her eyes shining with a mixture of excitement and fear.

"What have you got, Harper?" Olivia asked, her voice taut.

Natalie gestured to the large wall screen where she had projected the most critical documents. "Everything leads back to Volkov's network. Blueprints of a major U.S. city, potential targets, attack schedules – it's all here."

Elena leaned forward, her keen eyes scanning the material. "My God," she breathed. "If this is accurate..."

"Thousands of lives could be at stake," Olivia finished, her mouth set in a grim line. She exchanged a weighted look with Elena, the gravity of the situation settling squarely on their shoulders.

Turning back to the analyst, Olivia asked, "How certain are you about this intelligence, Natalie?"

Natalie met her gaze steadily. "One hundred percent, ma'am. I've triple-checked everything; this is real, and it's happening soon."

Olivia nodded, her mind already racing through possible courses of action. "Alright, Elena, get Jack Tanner in here. Natalie, I need you to keep digging. Find us everything you can on the specifics of this attack. We're going to need every scrap of information we can get."

As Elena rushed out to call Jack, Olivia turned back to the screen, her eyes tracing the lines of the city layout. She pushed aside the magnitude of what they were facing, even as it momentarily threatened to overwhelm her. There would be time for fear later. Right now, they had work to do.

OLIVIA RAINES STOOD at the head of the table, surveying her assembled team as the command center hummed with nervous energy. Jack Tanner, though disheveled, had arrived looking alert, his sharp eyes absorbing the data displayed on the surrounding screens. Beside him, Elena Salazar stood with a rigid, focused posture. At the far end of the table, Natalie Harper continued to work feverishly at her computer, streams of data reflecting off her glasses.

"Alright, people," Olivia said, her voice cutting through the subdued murmur of conversation. "We're working against the clock. Natalie, walk us through what you've found. We have a critical threat on our hands."

Natalie nodded and moved to stand before the large screen. "At approximately 0200 hours, I discovered a concealed cache of encrypted messages within the yacht logs we recovered. These messages directly link to a planned terrorist attack on American soil and contain detailed plans for a significant weapons deal."

She tapped a few keys, and a series of coded messages appeared on the screen. "From what we've been able to decipher so far, the weapons are scheduled to arrive at a U.S. port within the next 48 hours. The encryption is sophisticated, but I've managed to crack portions of it."

Jack leaned forward, his brow furrowed. "Any idea which port?"

Natalie shook her head. "Not yet. That's still buried in one of the deeper layers of encryption, but I'm working on it."

Elena spoke up, her voice tense with urgency. "We need to expedite this process. I can reach out to our FBI contacts, get their cyber specialists involved. Maybe they can help us crack this faster."

Olivia nodded her approval. "Do it. We need all hands on deck for this one."

As Elena turned away to make the call, Jack approached the screen, his eyes scanning the partially decoded texts. Pointing to a specific segment of code, he remarked, "Wait a second. That phrase there – 'Poseidon's Trident' – I've seen that before in some of our intelligence reports. It's been used as a code name for major East Coast ports."

Natalie's eyes lit up. "I'll cross-reference that with our database. That could be the key we need to narrow down the location."

The tension in the room ratcheted up with each passing minute as the team worked. Olivia paced back and forth, her mind churning through potential outcomes and contingency plans. She felt the full weight of what they were dealing with. If they failed, the consequences would be catastrophic.

Suddenly, Natalie let out a triumphant shout. "I've got it! The final layer of encryption just broke."

She pulled up the decoded message, and the team gathered around her screen. "The package is scheduled to arrive at the Port of Baltimore in exactly 43 hours and 17 minutes."

A collective gasp filled the room as the gravity of the situation sank in. They had less than two days to prevent a major terrorist attack.

Olivia straightened, her eyes blazing with determination. "Okay, folks. We know the what, where, and when. Now we need to figure out the how."

THE NEXT SEVERAL HOURS passed in a whirlwind of intense planning and preparation. Olivia led her team with laser-like focus, standing at the center of the storm.

"Elena," she said, "I need you to coordinate with the FBI and local law enforcement in Baltimore. We'll need their full cooperation, but we have to keep this under wraps. The last thing we need is for Volkov's people to catch wind of our operation."

Elena nodded briskly and immediately reached for her secure phone. "I'll set up a covert task force. I have some reliable contacts in the Baltimore PD."

Olivia turned to Jack. "Tanner, I want you to draw up a tactical plan for the port. We need to be ready for every contingency. Assume Volkov's men will be heavily armed and prepared for resistance."

Jack's eyes gleamed with a mix of excitement and deadly purpose. "You got it, boss. I'll have a full operational plan ready in two hours."

"Make it one," Olivia countered. "We don't have a second to waste."

As Jack rushed off to begin his planning, Olivia approached Natalie, who was still hunched over her computer. "Harper, you're our eyes and ears on this. I need you to keep digging into those files. Find us everything you can about the players involved, the weapons being shipped, any backup plans Volkov might have in place."

Natalie looked up, her eyes red-rimmed from hours of staring at screens, but her voice was steady. "Consider it done. By the time we move out, I'll have a full dossier ready."

Olivia squeezed her shoulder in silent gratitude, then turned back to the center of the room. She took a deep breath, feeling the weight of authority settle over her. The fate of countless innocent lives would be decided in the next forty-three hours. Failure was not an option.

As the team continued their frenzied preparations, Olivia allowed herself a moment of quiet reflection. She considered all the events that had led to this moment: the yacht massacre, Andrei Volkov's relentless pursuit, countless hours of research and analysis. It all came down to this.

Her reverie was interrupted by a sudden commotion. Jack had returned, his face flushed with anger, arguing heatedly with one of the younger team members.

"Are you out of your mind?" Jack was saying, his voice rising. "We'll tip off Volkov's men before we even get close to the cargo. We can't just waltz into the port guns blazing!"

Rodriguez, the junior agent, stood his ground. "And your plan is any better? Sneaking around in the shadows while a weapon of mass destruction sits right under our noses? We need to hit them hard and fast!"

Olivia strode over quickly to intervene, her voice slicing through the argument like a knife. "Enough! Both of you, stand down."

Though the tension between the two men remained palpable, they fell silent. Olivia fixed them each with a sharp glare. "We are a team, and we will act like one. We are facing a threat that could cost thousands of innocent lives. I understand that tensions are high, but we cannot afford to be at each other's throats. Is that clear?"

Both men nodded, looking slightly abashed. Olivia continued, her voice softening slightly. "Jack, I want to hear your plan. Rodriguez, you'll assist him. Sometimes the best strategy comes from a combination of approaches. Now, let's focus on what's important – stopping this attack and bringing Volkov down."

As the two men headed off to collaborate, Elena approached Olivia, a concerned expression on her face. "That was well handled," she said softly. "But Olivia, I can see the strain this is putting on you. Are you holding up okay?"

Olivia sighed, allowing a rare moment of vulnerability to show. "I'd be lying if I said I wasn't feeling the pressure, Elena. The stakes have never been higher."

Elena nodded, her eyes sympathetic. "I know. But if anyone can lead us through this, it's you. We all believe in you, Olivia. Don't forget that."

Olivia felt a surge of gratitude for her friend and colleague. "Thanks, Elena. That means more than you know."

With renewed determination, Olivia turned back to the task at hand. They had a terrorist attack to stop; time was running out.

AS THE SUN BEGAN TO set over the city, casting long shadows across the bustling Baltimore harbor, Olivia Raines and her team took their positions. Tension permeated the air, each team member acutely aware of the enormous stakes of their mission.

Olivia's voice crackled over the secure comm line. "All units, check in."

The team responded one by one:

"Tanner here. Tactical unit in position near the main entry point."

"Elena reporting. Local law enforcement is on standby, ready to move on our signal."

"Natalie checking in from the mobile command center. All systems are go. I have real-time contact with every team member."

Olivia nodded to herself, satisfied. "Alright, people. We know the shipment is due to arrive within the hour. Stay alert, stay focused, and remember – we're not just stopping a weapons deal tonight. We're preventing a catastrophe."

As night fell, the harbor took on an ominous character. The usual buzz of activity had ceased, leaving an unsettling silence broken only by the soft lapping of waves against the piers and the distant hum of city life.

Olivia scanned the main shipping channel, her pulse quickening with anticipation. Beside her, Elena kept a close eye on the few remaining dock workers, ready to signal if any showed signs of unusual activity.

"Natalie," Olivia said into her comm, "any update on the ship's approach?"

"Nothing yet," came the reply, tinged with frustration. "But our intel is solid. It should be here any– wait!" There was a pause, then Natalie's voice came back, urgent and excited. "I've got something on the radar. ETA five minutes. A cargo ship matching the description from our intel is approaching the port."

Olivia felt a surge of adrenaline. "This is it, people. Get ready."

The team waited, coiled like springs, ready to act. The next few minutes seemed to stretch into eternity. Finally, the ship appeared, a dark silhouette against the night sky.

"All units," Olivia said, her voice steady despite the tension thrumming through her body, "prepare to move on my signal. Remember, we need to secure that shipment and apprehend as many of Volkov's men as possible. But our primary objective is to prevent those weapons from leaving this port. Is that clear?"

A chorus of affirmatives sounded over the comm.

Olivia watched intently as the ship docked and the first of the crew began to disembark. She observed a group of dock workers approaching the ship, their movements slightly too deliberate, a little too rehearsed to be ordinary.

"Tanner," she said softly, "those dock workers. I think they're our guys."

"Copy that," Jack replied. "We see them. Ready to move on your go."

Olivia took a deep breath, centering herself for what was to come. Then, as the suspicious dock workers began to unload a series of large, unmarked containers, she gave the order they had all been waiting for:

"All units, move in now!"

The port erupted into chaos. Jack's tactical team surged onto the pier, quickly surrounding the workers and the cargo. The air filled with shouts of surprise and anger, then almost immediately with the sharp crack of gunfire.

Jack's voice came over the radio, tense with concentration. "Shots fired! We have armed hostiles resisting!"

Weapons drawn, Olivia and Elena raced down from their vantage point. As they neared the scene of the firefight, Olivia spotted several figures attempting to flee to a waiting vehicle.

"Elena, with me!" Olivia called out, and the two women took off in pursuit.

The chase led them through a maze of shipping containers, the sound of gunfire and shouting growing increasingly distant behind them. Suddenly, one of the fleeing suspects turned and opened fire. Bullets pinged off metal mere inches from their heads, forcing Olivia and Elena to dive for cover behind a nearby container.

"FBI! Drop your weapons!" Elena shouted, but the only response was another volley of shots.

Olivia caught Elena's eye, a silent plan forming between them. With a nod, Elena provided covering fire while Olivia darted from behind the container, closing the gap to their assailants. She tackled one of the men swiftly, quickly disarming him and securing his wrists with zip ties.

Elena followed close behind, efficiently subduing the second suspect. As they caught their breath, Olivia's comm crackled to life with Jack's voice.

"Port secure. Shipment contained. We have several suspects in custody, but it appears some of the higher-ups managed to escape in the confusion."

A mixture of relief and frustration washed over Olivia. They had prevented the weapons from leaving the port, potentially saving countless lives. But the job wasn't finished. Not while Andrei Volkov remained at large.

"Good work, everyone," she said into her comm, her voice tinged with grim resolve. "But this isn't over. Not by a long shot."

As the sounds of approaching sirens filled the air and the port buzzed with police officers securing the area, Olivia gazed out over the dark expanse of the harbor. Somewhere out there, Volkov was planning his next move. And she would be ready for him.

The battle was won, but the war was far from over. As the adrenaline of the operation began to subside, Olivia felt the weight of what lay ahead settle over her. Tonight, they had averted a disaster. But tomorrow would bring new challenges, new threats to face.

With a deep breath, Olivia turned back to her team. There would be time for rest later. For now, they had work to do. Debriefings to conduct, evidence to process, leads to follow. The fight against Volkov and his network was far from over, but tonight had proven they were on the right track.

As she walked back towards the command center, Olivia allowed herself a small smile. They had dealt Volkov a significant blow tonight. And with every operation, every piece of intelligence gathered, they were getting closer to bringing him down for good.

The night was far from over, but for the first time in months, Olivia felt a glimmer of hope. They were making progress. And no matter what Volkov had planned next, she and her team would be ready to face it head-on.

With renewed determination, Olivia stepped into the command center, ready to lead her team into the next phase of their mission. The battle against Volkov was far from over, but tonight had proven they were more than up to the challenge.

Chapter 9: Partisan Loyalties

The command center was bathed in the gentle glow of monitors, accompanied by the faint hum of computers. Olivia Raines stood before a large screen, her brow furrowed in concentration as she examined the complex network of facts before her. Something was amiss; she could feel it in her bones, a niggling sensation that had been growing over the past few days.

"Natalie," Olivia called, her voice cutting through the subdued buzz of activity in the room. "I need you to examine these communication logs more closely. There's an inconsistent pattern here."

The team's resident IT expert, Natalie Harper, swiveled in her chair and began typing furiously. Her fingers danced over the keyboard as Olivia delved deeper into the encrypted texts that had caught her eye.

Tension mounted as the minutes ticked by. Olivia paced back and forth, her mind racing with possibilities. She glanced at Jack Tanner, seated in the corner, his expression a mask of cool professionalism. His demeanor unsettled her, though she couldn't pinpoint why.

Natalie's voice shattered the stillness. "Olivia, you need to see this."

The team gathered around Natalie's desk, their faces illuminated by the harsh glow of her monitor. Olivia's heart sank as Natalie revealed her findings. The decoded records showed that her trusted second-in-command, Jack Tanner, had been covertly corresponding with an unidentified source.

Olivia's gaze flicked to Jack, who sat transfixed, his expression a mixture of horror and resignation. The other team members exchanged worried glances, the air heavy with unspoken accusations and shattered trust.

"Jack," Olivia's voice was low and controlled, masking the turmoil of emotions roiling beneath the surface. "My office. Now."

The rest of the team remained behind, their hushed conversations providing a backdrop to the drama unfolding as Olivia and Jack withdrew to her office. Olivia closed the door behind them, the soft click of the latch echoing in the tense atmosphere like a gunshot.

For a moment, neither spoke. Olivia leaned against her desk, arms folded, her piercing gaze fixed on Jack. He stood before her, shoulders squared, his usual confidence replaced by a nervous defensiveness.

At last, Olivia spoke, her voice barely above a whisper: "Explain yourself."

Jack took a deep breath. "Olivia, I know how this looks, but you have to trust me. I've been in contact with a former intelligence officer who's been feeding us crucial information about Volkov's operations."

Olivia closed her eyes, her voice rising with each syllable as the anger and disappointment she'd been suppressing finally spilled out. "And you didn't think this was something you should share with the team? With me?"

Jack shot back, his own frustration bubbling to the surface: "I was trying to protect you! You were safer not knowing. This source... he's taking enormous risks to help us. I couldn't jeopardize that."

"That wasn't your call to make, Jack!" Olivia slammed her fist on the desk, causing Jack to flinch at the sharp sound. "We're supposed to be a team. Do you have any idea what this looks like? How am I supposed to trust you now? We don't keep secrets from each other, especially not something this big."

As years of pent-up anxieties and disappointments poured out, the argument intensified, their voices rising. Accusations flew back and forth, each word cutting deeper than the last.

"You think I wanted to keep this from you?" Jack's voice trembled with emotion. "Every day, I've had to carry this burden alone, knowing that one wrong move could get us all killed. I've been trying to keep us one step ahead of Volkov, to give us a fighting chance!"

Olivia paused, her anger giving way to a mixture of uncertainty and curiosity. "What do you mean, 'one step ahead'?"

Jack reached into his pocket and pulled out a small flash drive. "See for yourself, Olivia. This contains every piece of intelligence I've gathered from my source. You'll find that the information has already saved our lives multiple times."

With shaking hands, Olivia took the drive and plugged it into her computer. Her eyes widened as she scrolled through the files. It was all there: detailed reports of planned ambushes, intimate knowledge of Volkov's operations, and warnings about potential moles within law enforcement agencies.

"My God, Jack," Olivia whispered, the implications of what she was seeing slowly sinking in. "This... This changes everything."

Jack nodded gravely. "I'm sorry, Olivia. I never meant to betray your trust. I know I should have told you sooner, but I was afraid. Afraid of compromising the source, afraid of putting you in danger."

Olivia sank into her chair, her head spinning with the revelation. Looking up at Jack, she saw not the traitor she had moments ago, but the loyal friend and colleague she had known for years.

"We need to work together on this, Jack," she said softly, her voice calmer now. "We use this information as a team. No more secrets."

Jack visibly relaxed. "Agreed. From now on, complete transparency. I'll schedule regular briefings to share any new intelligence from my contact."

They shook hands, a silent understanding passing between them. Though it would take time to fully rebuild the trust that had been damaged, they both recognized that their shared mission was too important to let personal conflicts stand in the way.

When they emerged from the office, the rest of the team was waiting anxiously. Olivia addressed them, explaining the situation and outlining the new protocol. Despite lingering concerns and residual uncertainty, the team appreciated the honest communication and the potential advantages of having an inside source.

As the tension in the room began to dissipate, Olivia's phone buzzed. It was a message from the Coast Guard's chief medical examiner, Dr. Lila Shah. "New findings from the yacht massacre. You need to see this ASAP."

Olivia caught Jack's eye and nodded. Together, they headed for the forensics lab, where Dr. Shah was waiting.

The lab's sterile environment was a stark contrast to their recently charged surroundings. Dr. Shah, petite with piercing eyes and a no-nonsense demeanor, greeted them with a grim expression.

"I'm glad you're both here," she said, leading them to her workstation. "What I've discovered fundamentally alters our understanding of the attack."

Dr. Shah pulled up a series of images on her computer screen, each more graphic than the last. "The ballistics analysis and DNA results paint a clear picture. This was a highly coordinated, professional hit, not just a random act of violence or a robbery gone wrong. The patterns of injuries, the types of weapons used - this was the work of experts."

Jack and Olivia exchanged glances, the implications of this insight sinking in.

"There's more," Dr. Shah continued, pulling up a chemical analysis report. "I found traces of a rare toxin in some of the victims. It's a signature compound used by a particular faction within Volkov's syndicate."

Jack leaned in to examine the report. "I've heard rumors about this group. They're Volkov's elite cleaners, used for high-profile eliminations."

Olivia's mind raced, making connections. "So the yacht massacre wasn't just about sending a message, but also a targeted elimination. But who on that yacht did Volkov want dead so badly?"

As they discussed the implications of Dr. Shah's findings, the scope of Volkov's operations began to take shape. The yacht massacre was one brutal move in a complex game of power and control.

Armed with this new knowledge, Olivia and Jack returned to the command center to brief the team. The atmosphere had shifted: the earlier conflict replaced by a shared sense of purpose and determination.

Natalie Harper's fingers flew across her keyboard as she cross-referenced the forensic data with known Volkov associates. "I've identified several potential suspects involved in the massacre," she said, pulling up a series of profiles on the main screen.

Elena Salazar, the team's tactical operations specialist, studied the information intently. "We should focus our efforts on this faction within Volkov's syndicate," she suggested. "Set up surveillance. If we can crack this group, we might be able to unravel Volkov's entire network."

Jack nodded in agreement. "My source has provided some additional background that corroborates Dr. Shah's findings," he said, sharing the latest information he'd received.

As the team worked to map out the connections between the massacre, the upcoming arms deal, and the planned attack on American soil, patterns began to emerge. Key players were identified, potential targets highlighted.

Olivia watched her team work with pride. Despite their earlier strife, they had come together, each contributing their unique skills and perspectives to the task at hand.

"Alright, people," she said, calling their attention. "We have a lot of work ahead of us. Natalie, I want you focused on tracking these suspects. Set up advanced surveillance and secure our communication channels. Elena, work with Jack to develop a detailed operational plan to target this faction. Dr. Shah, prepare additional forensic kits and briefings for our field team. We need to be ready for any contingency."

As the team dispersed to their assigned tasks, Olivia pulled Jack aside. "I need you to liaise with local and federal law enforcement," she said. "Make sure our operation has all the support it needs."

Jack nodded, a determined look in his eyes. "Consider it done."

The next few hours were a flurry of activity as the team prepared for their next move. The command center hummed with energy, each member laser-focused on their work. Olivia moved from station to station, providing guidance, asking questions, ensuring every angle was covered.

As the day wore on, the pieces of their strategy began to fall into place. Key suspects were under surveillance, operational tactics were refined, and support from various law enforcement agencies was secured.

Finally, as evening approached, Olivia gathered the team for a final review of their plan. They gathered around the central table, their expressions a mix of exhaustion and determination.

"Okay, let's go over this one more time," Olivia began. "Our primary objective is to neutralize this threat and gather enough evidence to bring down Volkov's entire operation. We've identified the faction responsible for the yacht massacre; we believe they're key players in Volkov's upcoming weapons deal and the planned attack on U.S. soil."

She turned to Elena. "Walk us through the operational plan."

Elena stepped forward, pulling up a detailed map on the main screen. "We'll be conducting simultaneous raids on three locations," she said, highlighting the targets. "Based on the intel from Jack's source and our surveillance, we believe these are the main bases of operation for this faction."

Jack chimed in, "Local SWAT teams will provide backup at each location. FBI and Homeland Security are on standby for additional support if needed."

"I've set up real-time data feeds from our surveillance," Natalie added. "We'll be able to track any movement in or out of these locations and adjust our approach on the fly if necessary."

Dr. Shah spoke up, "I've prepared specialized forensic kits for each team. They're equipped to handle any chemical or biological agents we might encounter, given what we know about this faction's methods."

Olivia nodded, a swell of pride rising as she looked at her team. Despite their challenges, the betrayals and the uncertainty, they had come together when it mattered most.

"I know the past few days have been difficult," she continued, her voice heavy with emotion. "Look at us now. We've taken a potential disaster and turned it into an opportunity to strike a decisive blow against Volkov's organization. Our trust in each other was shaken, and for a moment it seemed like we might fall apart."

She paused, meeting each of her team members' eyes. "What we're about to do is dangerous. We're going up against some of the most ruthless criminals in the world. But I want you all to know that there's no one else I'd rather have by my side. We're more than just a team - we're a family. And together, there's nothing we can't overcome."

A hush fell over the room as Olivia's words sank in. Then, slowly, the group seemed to fill with resolve. Backs straightened, jaws set, eyes focused with determination.

Jack stepped forward, standing beside Olivia. "We've been chasing Volkov for months," he said. "Always one step behind, always reacting to his moves. But now, for the first time, we have a chance to get ahead of him. To strike first and strike hard. This is our moment, people. Let's make it count."

Elena held out her hand, a wry smile on her face. "For the record, I'm totally stealing that speech for my next motivational seminar."

A wave of laughter broke the tension, and Olivia felt a surge of affection for her colleagues. Together, they had been through hell; they had faced betrayals and disappointments. But here they were, ready to risk everything to protect their country and bring a dangerous criminal to justice.

"Alright, folks," Olivia said, her voice firm with resolve. "You know your roles. Get some rest, check your gear, and be ready to move out at 0500. Tomorrow, we take the fight to Volkov."

As the team dispersed to prepare for the coming challenge, Olivia remained in the command center. Standing before the large screen, she studied the faces of their targets and the maps of the operational sites. In her mind, she ran through every possible scenario, every potential complication.

Jack approached, carrying two mugs of coffee. Olivia accepted one gratefully.

"Second thoughts?" he asked, coming to stand beside her.

Olivia tilted her head. "No, just making sure we haven't overlooked anything. There's so much at stake."

Jack nodded, understanding. "We've done everything we can to prepare. The team is ready. You've led us this far, Olivia. Trust in that."

She turned to him, a small smile on her lips. "Funny how quickly things can change. A few days ago, I wasn't sure I could trust you at all."

"I'm sorry again for keeping secrets," Jack said softly. "I promise you, from now on, complete transparency."

Olivia placed a hand on his shoulder. "I know. And I'm sorry for doubting you. We've always been stronger together, Jack."

As they stood there, looking out over the quiet command center, Olivia felt a sense of calm settle over her. Though danger and uncertainty awaited them tomorrow, in this moment she knew with absolute clarity that they were ready to face whatever challenges lay ahead.

As the first light of dawn began to creep across the sky, they prepared to confront Volkov's network and end his reign of terror once and for all. The stage was set for a confrontation that would test their courage, skill, and the bonds that held them together. Whatever the outcome, Olivia knew they would face it not just as a team, but as a family.

Chapter 10: A Lethal Game

The Sentinel sliced through the waves with deliberate accuracy as it negotiated the stormy seas. Olivia Raines stood in the bow of the Coast Guard cutter, staring forward where a black smudge was gradually forming. Their destination, the far-off island, loomed before them like a lush fortification rising from the water, housing equal measures of secrets and threats.

Behind her, Elena Salazar and Jack Tanner were making last-minute arrangements with deliberate motions. Their objective hung heavy in the air, and every team member was sharply aware of the stakes. The ghost that had eluded them for so long, Andrei Volkov, was here. The key to undoing his evil intentions lay on this little patch of land and rock.

"Olivia," Natalie Harper's voice crackled over the comm link, "I have updated satellite images. There should be enough cover for your approach from a small cove on the northwest side of the island."

Olivia nodded, though Natalie couldn't see it. "Copy that. Any indication of activity?"

"Nothing obvious, but don't let that fool you. I'm detecting some unusual heat signatures deeper inland. Could be camouflaged buildings or equipment."

"Understood. Keep us advised on any changes."

Olivia turned to quickly inform her crew, then looked at Diego Ortega. The man stood somewhat apart from the others, his posture relaxed yet vigilant. His participation in this mission was a calculated risk; while his knowledge of Volkov's activities was invaluable, skepticism nevertheless loomed large. They couldn't afford the luxury of total trust.

"Alright, listen up," Olivia said, gathering her team around her. "We're here to gather intel and, if possible, disrupt Volkov's operation. This isn't a surgical strike. Stay alert, stay together, and remember—we're in hostile territory from the moment our feet touch sand." They had less than thirty minutes to prepare.

The squad nodded, their features a combination of focused concern and determination. Ever the soldier, Jack was already surveying the approaching coast. His thoughts were clearly charting tactical locations and potential hazards.

The quiet thrum of the engine faded as the Sentinel descended into the hidden cove. The squad disembarked quickly, their movements refined from countless training exercises and real operations. Olivia led her group toward the tree line, her boots sinking slightly into the damp sand.

Before them, the forest loomed, a wall of green that seemed to pulse with secret life. Olivia raised a clenched fist to signal a stop. "Establish a perimeter," she said in a hushed voice. "Elena, take our six. Jack, on my left. Diego, right flank."

An eerie silence enveloped the island as they formed their positions. No birds called, no insects buzzed—it was as if the whole atmosphere was waiting.

As they began their push into the dense undergrowth, Olivia felt a droplet of perspiration trickle down her spine. Every cracking twig and rustling leaf sent adrenaline coursing through her body. Volkov's soldiers could be anywhere, watching and waiting.

When Olivia's senses screamed a warning, they had covered about half a mile. Once again raising her hand, she halted the squad in its tracks. Ahead, just barely discernible through the dense foliage, something moved.

She said "Contact" softly into her comm. "Two o'clock, twenty meters."

With weapons at the ready, Jack and Elena moved in perfect flanking formations. Diego's gaze fixed on the spot Olivia had indicated, surprising her as he had already melted into the shadow of a large tree.

For a prolonged moment, nothing stirred. Then gunfire erupted like a thunderstorm amid the stifling calm. Muzzle flashes illuminated the dark undergrowth as Volkov's agents opened fire from concealed positions.

"Cover!" Olivia yelled, scrambling behind a fallen log. Splinters flew as bullets thudded against the crumbling timber. She returned fire, her shots precise even in the chaos.

Jack was a calm bastion to her left, carefully selecting targets with measured rounds from his rifle. Elena had ascended, using the natural elevation to rain down suppressing fire.

But it was Diego who truly astonished her. He maneuvered through the underbrush like a phantom, tracking the enemy positions. Two sharp cracks rang out, and the opposing fire immediately slackened.

"Clear!" Diego called, his voice a mixture of exhilaration and grim satisfaction.

As the echoes of gunfire faded and the island's eerie calm once again took center stage, Olivia sensed a shift in the team's dynamics. Diego's actions had spoken louder than any words of allegiance could have.

"Good work," she remarked, meeting Diego's eyes as the team regrouped. "That was some impressive shooting."

Diego nodded, a slight smile flickering at the corners of his lips. "I've had practice," he stated simply.

With the immediate danger eliminated, Olivia took stock of her team. There were minor cuts and bruises, but nothing serious. The real damage was to their element of surprise—Volkov would know they were here now.

"We need to move," Olivia said. "That patrol was just the beginning. Volkov will have the entire island on high alert."

As they ventured deeper into the island's interior, the terrain became increasingly treacherous. Steep hills and jagged rocks replaced the dense vegetation. Every step had to be carefully considered, every path scrutinized for signs of ambushes or traps.

Natalie's voice came through on the comm, a lifeline from the outside world. "Heads up, team. I'm picking up some odd readings about a quarter mile ahead. Could be camouflaged buildings or equipment caches."

Olivia acknowledged the warning, her mind racing through various scenarios. If Volkov had established a significant presence here, they might be approaching a hornet's nest.

The team's progress slowed as they encountered the first of Volkov's defensive measures. Jack's expertise proved invaluable as he discovered and disarmed a series of cleverly placed pressure-sensitive explosives hidden beneath innocent-looking piles of leaves, tripwires connected to claymore mines, and pit traps lined with sharpened stakes.

"These are professional grade," Jack said as he carefully removed a particularly nasty device. "Military-level ordnance, not something you'd pick up on the black market."

Olivia furrowed her brow. The implications were disturbing. If Volkov had access to this kind of equipment, his reach was far greater than they had imagined.

Diego's local knowledge became apparent as they negotiated a particularly difficult stretch of terrain, an almost vertical rock face slick with moss and moisture.

"There's an easier path," he said, indicating an almost imperceptible track snaking around the base of the cliff. "It's longer, but safer. Volkov's men use it to move heavy equipment."

Olivia studied Diego's face, searching for any sign of deception. Finding none, she nodded. "Lead the way."

The detour proved accurate; Olivia felt a wave of reluctant admiration for Diego when they emerged onto a small plateau. His intelligence was solid, his skills undeniable. Still, a small part of her remained wary, not yet ready to fully trust a man so deeply entrenched in Volkov's world.

The team paused to catch their breath and reorient themselves. Knowing the most challenging part of their mission still lay ahead, Olivia gathered her team.

"We're close," she said, her voice low but firm. "Everything we've fought for, every lead we've chased, it all comes down to what we find here. Volkov thinks he's untouchable on this island fortress of his. Let's prove him wrong."

As the sun began to sink toward the horizon, casting sharp oranges and deep purples across the sky, Olivia and her team finally glimpsed their target. Volkov's complex sat nestled in a natural bowl-shaped depression, sheltered on three sides by towering cliffs.

From their vantage point, Olivia could see the facility was a masterpiece of deception and camouflage. Partially submerged buildings sported living foliage on their rooftops that blended seamlessly with the surrounding forest. The hive of activity below was betrayed only by the occasional glint of metal or flicker of movement.

"Damn," Jack muttered, peering through his binoculars. "Place is a fortress. I count at least twenty armed guards on perimeter duty alone."

Elena, who had been studying the layout of the compound, gestured to a section of the eastern wall. "There," she said. "That looks like our best bet for entry. The vegetation is thicker, and the guard rotations seem to have a slight gap there."

Olivia nodded, already formulating a plan. "Agreed. Jack, you and the rest of the team will create a diversion at the main gate. Elena,

Diego, and I will use that window to slip inside. We'll need a distraction to draw attention away from that section."

As the team finalized details, Natalie's voice came through once more. "I've found a vulnerability in their surveillance network," she said. "You'll need to move quickly; I can cause a temporary blackout in their systems, but it won't last long."

With roles defined and the agenda set, Olivia felt a familiar tension coiling in her gut. Months of preparation, countless close calls, and sacrifices beyond measure would either pay off or come crashing down around them in the next few moments.

"Remember," she said, meeting each team member's eyes in turn, "we're not here to take on the entire compound. Get in, gather what intel we can, and get out. If we can deal some damage to their operation in the process, all the better."

As the last light faded from the sky, plunging the island into darkness broken only by the soft glow from the facility below, Olivia gave the signal. Jack and his group positioned themselves to unleash calculated chaos on the main entrance.

Olivia, Elena, and Diego crept toward their entry point, every sense on high alert. Moments later, Jack's diversionary attack came—a symphony of gunfire, shouts, and explosions shattering the night's quiet.

"Now!" Olivia hissed, and the three sprinted for the gap in the perimeter defenses. Natalie's promised blackout came right on cue, plunging the eastern section of the complex into darkness.

Moving swiftly and silently, they slipped inside like ghosts. Olivia's heart pounded in her chest, adrenaline surging through her veins as she navigated the labyrinthine interior of Volkov's stronghold.

Their first stroke of luck came in the form of a command center, its door left ajar in the chaos of the attack. Inside, computer displays glowed softly, a wealth of intelligence waiting to be harvested.

Elena set to work immediately, her camera clicking rapidly to capture images of maps and documents scattered across a large table. Diego moved with surprising efficiency, copying data from the computer terminals onto a portable drive.

Olivia pored over a series of detailed plans, her eyes widening. The scope of Volkov's planned strike was staggering—multiple targets spread across several countries, timed to create maximum devastation and chaos.

"My God," she breathed, her finger tracing the list of targets. "If even half of this comes to pass..."

Shaking off the momentary paralysis, knowing every second counted, she keyed her comm. "Natalie, are you getting this?"

"Coming through loud and clear," Natalie confirmed, her voice tight with anxiety. "This is big, Olivia. Bigger than we imagined."

As Elena and Diego finished gathering everything they could, Olivia moved quickly, reaching into her rucksack for a set of compact explosive charges.

"We're not just leaving with intel," she said, rapidly placing the charges at key structural points throughout the room. "We're going to seriously disrupt Volkov's operations while we're here."

The team was ready to exfiltrate, the explosives set on a timer. But their luck had run out. As they turned back into the hallway, shouts and the pounding of boots on metal floors indicated that Volkov's forces had regrouped and were sweeping the facility.

"Move!" Olivia ordered, leading her group down a side passage. They sprinted, the sounds of pursuit growing louder behind them.

As they rounded a corner, the first bullets whizzed past, forcing them to take cover behind a series of large storage containers. Olivia returned fire, her shots accurate even in the chaos.

"We need an exit!" Elena shouted above the din of gunfire.

It was Diego who found the solution. "This way!" he called, pointing to a maintenance hatch. "It leads to an underground tunnel system; we can use it to bypass their defenses!"

Olivia hesitated for a split second, weighing the risk of trusting Diego against their rapidly dwindling options. "Do it!" she decided.

Elena provided covering fire as Olivia and Diego wrenched open the hatch. They descended one by one into the darkness below, the sounds of battle muffled but still too close for comfort.

Though the tunnels were a maze of dead ends and winding passages, Diego navigated them with unerring precision. Olivia realized his knowledge of Volkov's operation went far beyond what he had initially let on.

"How did you know about these?" she demanded as they ran.

A massive explosion rocked the entire facility, cutting off Diego's reply. Olivia's charges had detonated, turning the command center into a fiery inferno.

"Later!" Diego yelled. "We need to move!"

Emerging from the tunnels near their initial landing site, they could hear chaos from the complex echoing across the island. In the distance, Olivia spotted the welcome sight of the Sentinel approaching the shore.

Still, their escape was far from certain. Enraged by the destruction of their base, Volkov's soldiers mounted a fierce counterattack. As they raced toward the extraction spot, bullets pounded sand all around them.

Diego really showed his value in these last, desperate hours. Diego positioned himself defensively, throwing down suppressing fire to drive off the assailants while Olivia and Elena headed for the boat.

He yelled, his gun booming in measured spurts. "Go!" "I'll cover you!"

Olivia paused, reluctant to part from a team member—even one whose allegiance had been called into doubt. She cried back, "Not without you!"

They struggled their way to the waiting boat together. Jack covered fire from the Sentinel's deck after reorganizing with the evacuation crew.

The whole weight of what they had achieved started to seep in as they climbed on. They had seriously disrupted Volkov's operation and fled carrying information that would destroy his whole network.

Rising to life, the Sentinel's engines drove them far from the island and left anarchy in their path. Olivia turned back toward the fading beach, where the compound's fires still illuminated the night sky.

"We did it," Elena murmured, sounding a combination of weariness and excitement.

Olivia nodded and smiled slightly. "We did; but this is only the beginning. Volkov is wounded, but not defeated. Now he knows we're coming for him."

Olivia glanced to Diego as the island sank into night behind them. She could wait for her queries about his background, his actual loyalty. She just held out her hand right now.

"Thank you," she remarked just now. "We could not have done this without you."

Diego grabbed her hand and looked at her with fresh clarity. He said, "I'm where I need to be."

Olivia let herself a minute of calm contemplation as the Sentinel sliced over the seas, dragging them back to a world that had no clue how near it had come to calamity. Though the struggle against Volkov and his network was far from over, they had won a pivotal fight.

Olivia focused on the difficulties ahead, the weight of the pilfers intelligence in her pack and the determination of her crew strengthened by their achievement driving her. Though Volkov had been outmatched today, she understood the game was far from over. His would be the next action; they must be ready.

Chapter 11: The Very Ultimate Deception

Olivia Raines hunched over her desk, her face softly illuminated by the glow of computer displays. The clock on her office wall ticked past midnight, but sleep was far from her mind. An uneasy feeling gnawed at her core.

For weeks, minor anomalies had been nagging at her. Projects that should have proceeded smoothly encountered unexpected resistance. Targets seemed to vanish just before her squad could reach them. Somehow, Volkov's network always managed to stay one step ahead.

Olivia's fingers flew across the keyboard, cross-referencing mission details with intercepted Volkov communications. As the pieces began to align, a chill crept up her spine. The truth was undeniable, yet almost too horrifying to contemplate.

There was a mole in her team.

She leaned back in her chair, massaging her temples as she grappled with the implications. Someone she trusted, someone she had personally selected for this crucial mission, had betrayed them all. The realization made her blood boil, but she knew she couldn't act on instinct alone. She needed a strategy and hard evidence.

Over the next three days, Olivia scrutinized her staff with heightened vigilance, searching for any hint of suspicious behavior or deceit. She analyzed every keystroke, every glance, every interaction. But whoever the traitor was, they were skilled at covering their tracks.

During their next team meeting, Olivia decided to set a trap. As they discussed their upcoming operations, she subtly inserted a piece of false information—a decoy target, a fabricated vulnerability in Volkov's defenses. She watched closely for any reaction, but her staff remained professional and focused.

It wasn't until later that evening, as she monitored their secure communication channels, that Olivia saw the bait being taken. A heavily encrypted message containing the planted information was transmitted from their network. Her heart sank as she traced the source of the communication.

Lieutenant Harris. One of her most trusted operatives.

The following morning, Olivia summoned Harris to her office. As he entered, she closed the door behind him, ensuring their privacy. Harris took a seat across from her desk, raising an eyebrow but remaining silent.

"We need to talk, Michael," Olivia said, her voice firm despite the turmoil within her.

Harris leaned back, his posture relaxed. "What's on your mind, boss?"

Olivia fixed him with an unwavering gaze. "How long have you been feeding Volkov information? I think you know exactly what's on my mind."

A flicker of fear crossed Harris's face before he regained his composure. "Is this some kind of joke, Olivia? I have no idea what you're talking about."

"Do I look like I'm joking?" Olivia replied with icy clarity. She turned her computer screen towards Harris, displaying the intercepted message. "Care to explain this?"

Harris stared at the screen, the color draining from his face. For a long moment, silence hung heavy in the room. Then, like a dam breaking, words poured from him.

"You don't understand," he said, his voice cracking. "They have my family. Volkov... he threatened to kill them if I didn't cooperate. What was I supposed to do?"

Olivia felt a conflicting surge of compassion and anger. She had known Harris for years, had trusted him with her life on numerous occasions. While she could see the genuine anguish in his eyes, the betrayal still stung.

"Why didn't you come to me?" she asked, her voice softening slightly. "We could have extracted your family, protected them."

Harris shook his head, his shoulders slumping in defeat. "I thought if I just gave Volkov enough to keep him satisfied, I could keep everyone safe. I never meant for it to go this far." He looked up, his eyes haunted. "Volkov's reach seemed endless."

Olivia stood behind her desk, weighing her options. While she couldn't excuse Harris's actions, she also couldn't bring herself to throw him to the wolves. More importantly, she saw an opportunity to turn the tables on Volkov.

"Here's what's going to happen," she said at last, silencing Harris with a sharp look. "You're going to be placed under guard, but you're also going to continue communicating with Volkov. Only this time, you'll be feeding him the information we want him to have. Do you understand?"

Harris nodded, his expression a mix of relief and apprehension. "I want to make this right, Olivia. I'll do whatever you need me to do."

As Harris was being escorted away by security, Olivia summoned Elena Salazar and Jack Tanner to her office. Now more than ever, she needed her most loyal lieutenants.

"We have a situation," she said when they arrived, quickly bringing them up to speed on Harris's betrayal and her plan to use him as a double agent.

Elena's eyes flashed with anger. "I can't believe Harris would do this. How can we trust anything he does now?"

"We can't," Olivia said. "But this is also an opportunity. If we play this right, we can feed Volkov exactly what we want him to believe. We'll be monitoring his every move."

Jack nodded slowly. "It's risky, but it could give us the edge we need. We'll have to be careful though – one slip and Volkov will know we're onto him."

Their discussion of the specifics of their new strategy was interrupted by a knock on the door. Admiral Marcus Blackwell entered, his expression grim.

"Olivia, we need to talk," he said, nodding for Elena and Jack to leave. After they exited, Blackwell sank into a chair, looking more worn than Olivia had ever seen him.

"I just got off the phone with Senator Raines," he said, rubbing his forehead. "He's demanding results, Olivia. The political pressure is mounting, and I'm running out of ways to buy you time."

Olivia felt a knot forming in her stomach. Her own father, Senator Richard Raines, had never approved of her career path. Now it seemed he was using his political clout to interfere with her mission.

"We're making progress, Admiral," she said, leaning forward. "We've just uncovered a significant lead. If we rush this, we risk losing everything we've worked for."

Blackwell sighed heavily. "I understand that, Olivia. But my hands are increasingly tied. We need to show some concrete results, and soon. Otherwise, I may be forced to pull the plug on this operation."

As Blackwell departed, Olivia felt the weight of responsibility settling on her shoulders. Though she had always known this mission would be challenging, today it felt as if she was fighting battles on every front.

Reassembling her team, Olivia steeled herself for the difficult conversation ahead. She watched a range of emotions play across their faces as she explained the situation with Harris and the mounting political pressure: shock, anger, betrayal, and finally, determination.

"I know this is a lot to process," Olivia said, "but we can't let this derail us. We're closer than ever to stopping Volkov, and I need every one of you focused and united."

Natalie Harper, their IT specialist, stood up. "We should review all of our communication systems. If Harris was compromised, we need to ensure there are no other vulnerabilities."

Olivia nodded in agreement. "Good thinking, Natalie. Jack, Elena – I want you to help me devise a strategy for using Harris as a double agent. We have one shot at this, and we need to make it count."

As the team dispersed to work, Olivia felt reinvigorated with a newfound sense of purpose. Though they had suffered a significant setback, they were far from defeated. If anything, this challenge had only sharpened their resolve.

Over the next several days, Olivia's office became the nerve center of their operation. Maps, schematics, and data streams covered every available surface as they meticulously crafted their deception.

"We need to feed Volkov information that's believable but ultimately misleading," Olivia said, gesturing to a map of suspected Volkov holdings. "We'll give him just enough truth to make the lies palatable."

Elena nodded, her analytical mind already racing ahead. "We could leak information about a planned raid here," she said, indicating one site. "But in reality, we'll be focusing on this facility instead."

While they refined their approach, Olivia brought in a heavily guarded Harris to brief him on his role. The weight of his actions clearly bore heavily on him, but there was also a glint of determination in his eyes—a desire for redemption.

"Every word, every inflection matters," Olivia warned him. "Volkov will be scrutinizing everything you say. One misstep, and this all falls apart."

Harris nodded gravely. "I understand. I won't let you down again, Olivia."

The team held its collective breath as Harris made his first controlled contact with Volkov's network. Natalie's fingers flew across the keyboard, tracking every bit of data sent and received. As they waited for Volkov's response, the tension in the room was palpable.

Hours passed, feeling like an eternity. Then, finally, a breakthrough.

"We've got movement!" Natalie exclaimed, her eyes fixed on the screen. "Volkov's network is reacting to the false intel. They're redirecting resources, just as we predicted."

A cautious cheer went up from the team. It was working as planned. With doubt successfully sown in Volkov's mind, they set their next phase into motion.

Though Olivia knew this was just the beginning, she allowed herself a small smile of satisfaction. The real test was yet to come. As she surveyed her team, their features a mix of exhaustion and exhilaration, she felt a wave of pride. Despite everything they had been through, they had come together when it mattered most.

"Good work, everyone," she said, genuine gratitude in her voice. "But let's not celebrate just yet. We've opened the door; now we need to be ready to walk through it."

As the team dispersed to prepare for the next stage of their operation, Olivia found herself alone in her office. She gazed out the window at the city lights below, her mind racing with possibilities and potential pitfalls.

They had taken an enormous risk in turning Harris into a double agent. They were feeding Volkov a delicate balance of truth and deception. One mistake, one piece of information that didn't quite fit, and their entire strategy could come crashing down around them.

Further complicating an already precarious situation was the political pressure from Senator Raines and waning support from Admiral Blackwell. Olivia knew they were running out of time. They needed to strike at Volkov's network decisively and soon.

Her thoughts were interrupted by a soft knock on the door. Elena entered, carrying two steaming mugs of coffee.

"Thought you could use this," Elena said, handing Olivia a cup. "You've barely slept in days."

Olivia inhaled the rich aroma of the coffee gratefully. "Thanks. I'm not sure I even remember what sleep feels like right now."

Elena leaned against the desk, studying Olivia's face. "How are you holding up? Really?"

For a moment, Olivia considered brushing off the question with her usual assurance that she was fine. But under Elena's steady gaze, her defenses crumbled.

"Honestly? I'm terrified," Olivia said, her voice barely above a whisper. "We're walking such a fine line here. If we fail, Volkov will know exactly what we're doing, and the consequences would be catastrophic."

Elena nodded, understanding etched on her face. "You're not carrying this alone, Olivia. We're all in this together. It's a heavy burden."

Olivia felt a lump in her throat, touched by Elena's unwavering support. "I just hope it's enough. I know I couldn't ask for a better team."

As dawn broke over the city, casting a soft light through the office windows, Olivia and Elena continued to talk, refining their plans and weighing every possible outcome. Though danger lay ahead, they were prepared to face it head-on.

In the days that followed, the team worked tirelessly to build on their initial success. Harris continued to feed carefully crafted misinformation to Volkov's network, while Olivia and her team monitored the ripple effects of their deception.

They watched as Volkov's operations began to show signs of strain. Shipments were rerouted, meetings called off, and a clear paranoia began to develop within the criminal network. Though Olivia knew they couldn't afford to become complacent, it was clear their strategy was working.

"We need to push harder," she told her team during a strategy session. "Volkov's off-balance, but he's not down yet. We need to deliver a knockout blow."

Jack Tanner leaned forward, concentration furrowing his brow. "What if we set up a sting operation? Use the intel we've been feeding them to lure out some of Volkov's top lieutenants?"

Olivia nodded, her mind already spinning with possibilities. "It's risky, but it could work. If we can take out a significant portion of his command structure, it might be enough to topple his entire operation."

Even as they worked out the details of their plan, Olivia felt uneasy. She knew they were pushing their luck. Each move they made increased their level of exposure. But with pressure mounting from all sides, they had no choice but to press on.

Late one night, as Olivia pored over the latest intelligence reports, her secure line rang. It was Admiral Blackwell.

"We have a problem," he said without preamble, his voice tight with tension. "Senator Raines is questioning our methods, our results... everything. He's making noise about launching a formal inquiry into our operation."

Olivia felt a surge of frustration and anger. Her father had always opposed her career choice, but this felt like a personal attack. "What are our options?"

Blackwell sighed heavily. "We need a big win, Olivia. Something we can point to that justifies all the time and resources we've invested. Otherwise, I'm not sure how much longer I can keep this operation running."

As she hung up the phone, Olivia's mind raced. They were so close to bringing down Volkov's network. But now, with the threat of governmental intervention looming, their window of opportunity was rapidly closing.

Once again gathering her team, Olivia laid out the situation bluntly. "We're out of time," she said, meeting each of their eyes squarely. "We need to launch the sting operation we've been planning. Now."

Chapter 12: The Trap

Andrei Volkov's subterranean command center flickered with harsh fluorescent light, casting an unsettling glow on his top lieutenants' faces. Tension permeated the room as Volkov, his steel-gray eyes scrutinizing everything, leaned forward on the polished mahogany table.

"We have a unique opportunity before us," he growled, his deep voice demanding instant attention. "Our little mole has been feeding false information to Olivia Raines and her team. Now, it's time to set our trap."

The room buzzed with anticipation. Volkov's reputation for mercilessness was well-known, and his agents understood that whatever strategy he had in mind would be both cunning and terrible.

"We're going to disseminate rumors of a significant arms deal," Volkov continued, a nasty smirk playing at the corners of his lips. "An abandoned warehouse on the outskirts of the city. Too tempting for Raines to overlook."

Volkov's lieutenants nodded in agreement as he outlined the specifics of his strategy, their eyes gleaming with a mixture of respect and fear. Within hours, Volkov's network was buzzing with meticulously crafted false information, each piece designed to lure Olivia Raines into a deadly web.

Miles away, in a nondescript office building serving as a front for her clandestine activities, Olivia Raines hunched over her computer, her brow furrowed in concentration. A tip had come through one of her most trusted sources: a large shipment of firearms was due to arrive at an abandoned warehouse in less than 24 hours.

"Natalie," Olivia called, her voice taut with urgency, "I need satellite imagery of this location. Now."

Natalie Harper's fingers flew over the keyboard, bringing up the requested images on the main screen. "Nothing unusual showing up, Olivia," she reported, a note of concern in her voice. "It appears to be completely abandoned."

Olivia leaned back in her chair, scrutinizing the images, her green eyes narrowing. Something felt off, but she couldn't quite put her finger on it. Though her instincts screamed caution, the opportunity was too good to pass up.

"Get the team together," she decided, pushing away from her desk. "We move out in one hour."

As the team assembled, Olivia briefed them on the situation. Elena Salazar listened intently, her years of experience as a DEA agent evident in the incisive questions she posed. Her black hair was pulled back in a tight ponytail. Jack Tanner, a former Navy SEAL and weapons expert, was already mentally running through possible scenarios, his muscular frame tense with anticipation. Their tech specialist, Marco Fernades, busied himself with their communication equipment, ensuring they'd have a secure link throughout the operation.

"I don't like it," Elena stated bluntly as Olivia finished. "It feels too easy."

Olivia nodded, acknowledging the concern. "I agree, but we can't afford to let this opportunity slip by. If Volkov is moving weapons on this scale, we need to know about it."

"What's our play?" Jack asked, his voice stern but tinged with barely contained excitement.

"We go in quiet," Olivia replied, her tone brooking no argument. "Full stealth approach. If it's legitimate, we gather intel and get out. If it's a trap..." She paused, looking around at her team. "We're ready for anything."

As the squad geared up, Olivia felt the familiar surge of adrenaline coursing through her veins. She lived for this: the thrill of the chase, the chance to bring down one of the most dangerous criminals on the planet. Yet, beneath the excitement, a persistent unease lingered. Was she leading her team into danger?

The night was moonless, a black canvas shrouding the city as Olivia's team headed toward the warehouse. The tactical vehicle glided silently through empty streets, its occupants tense and alert.

Jack broke the silence, his eyes fixed on the thermal imaging device. "No heat signatures in the immediate vicinity," he murmured. "It's quiet. Too quiet."

In the back, Elena and Diego quietly discussed entry points and escape routes. Though Olivia could sense the underlying tension, their tones remained cool and professional.

"We park here," Olivia announced as they neared their target. "We proceed on foot from this point. Radio silence unless absolutely necessary."

The team moved like shadows, their dark clothing blending with the night. Olivia took point, her senses heightened, every muscle in her body coiled and ready for action. As they approached the perimeter of the warehouse, she raised a hand, signaling the team to halt.

Using hand gestures, she assigned roles. Elena would enter with her, while Jack and Diego covered their flanks. As they prepared to move in, Olivia couldn't shake the feeling that they were walking into something far deadlier than they had anticipated.

The warehouse loomed before them, a hulking mass of broken glass and corrugated metal. Weapons drawn, Olivia and Elena approached the main entrance. With a nod to Elena, Olivia grasped the door handle, her heart pounding in her chest.

The door creaked open, revealing a cavernous interior shrouded in darkness. This was ominous. Long shadows cast by abandoned equipment and crates created a maze of potential hiding spots. Inching forward, Olivia and Elena scanned for any sign of movement—any trace of the expected weapons shipment.

An eerie stillness descended as the team spread out through the warehouse, searching. The only sounds were their own muffled footsteps and the occasional creak of metal settling in the night air.

Suddenly, a sharp crack echoed through the warehouse. Olivia's eyes widened in realization. "It's a trap!" she shouted, but her warning came too late.

A series of explosions rocked the structure, the concussive force throwing Olivia off her feet. Disoriented, her ears ringing from the blast, she scrambled for cover behind a stack of crates. The air was thick with dust and reeked of explosives.

Before she could fully regain her bearings, the warehouse erupted in gunfire. Muzzle flashes illuminated the darkness as Volkov's men—who had been lying in wait—opened up with automatic weapons.

Olivia's training kicked in; her body moved on instinct as she returned fire, her shots precise despite the chaos around her. "Elena!" she yelled over the din. "Status!"

"I'm okay!" Elena's voice came from somewhere to her left. "Heavy fire coming from the north side!"

Olivia could hear Jack and Diego engaging the threat, their voices rising in a mix of shouts and curses above the cacophony of battle.

The firefight was intense; bullets splintering wood and ricocheting off metal surfaces. Olivia's mind raced through their options. Caught in a well-executed ambush, they were outnumbered and outgunned. Staying to fight would only result in more casualties.

"Fall back!" Olivia shouted, her voice cutting through the mayhem. "We're getting out of here!"

Elena responded immediately, laying down suppressing fire to cover their retreat. Jack appeared, half-carrying an injured team member, his face a mask of grim determination.

"Diego!" Olivia called out. "We need an exit!"

Diego's voice crackled over their radios. "We might have our best shot through a series of passages to the east!"

As they regrouped, Olivia could see the toll the ambush had taken on her squad. Though battered and bloodied, their eyes still blazed with determination. She felt a wave of guilt mixed with pride in their resilience, remorse for leading them into this trap.

"This way!" Diego shouted, pointing toward a narrow corridor almost hidden by a pile of rusty machinery.

With Diego in the lead, they moved swiftly, navigating the labyrinthine warehouse passages. The echoes of pursuit spurred them on. Just when they thought they might have found a clear path to escape, they rounded a corner to find another group of Volkov's agents blocking their route.

Time seemed to slow as both parties raised their weapons. In that split-second, Olivia made a decision. She reached for her belt and pulled out a flashbang grenade.

"Eyes!" she yelled in warning to her team, then hurled the grenade at their attackers.

Even with their eyes closed and ears covered, the subsequent blast of light and sound was disorienting. But it bought them the precious seconds they needed. As Volkov's men stumbled, temporarily blinded and deafened, Olivia and her team rushed past them, bursting out a side door into the cool night air.

They kept running until they were several blocks away, the sounds of chaos at the warehouse fading into the distance. Only then did they allow themselves to slow, gasping for air, the reality of their narrow escape sinking in.

"Everyone okay?" Olivia asked, scanning her team for injuries.

Nods and whispered affirmations followed. Though far from unscathed, they were alive. As they made their way to their designated safehouse, the weight of the evening's events settled heavily on their shoulders.

The safehouse was a nondescript apartment in a quiet neighborhood, chosen for its anonymity. As they poured in, the adrenaline of their escape began to fade, replaced by pain and exhaustion.

"Lila's on her way," Olivia announced, referring to Dr. Lila Shah, the Coast Guard's top medical examiner who moonlighted as their team doctor. "She'll be here soon to patch us up."

While they waited, Olivia and Elena began to debrief, their voices low and intense.

"He knew we were coming," Elena muttered, dark eyes flashing with anger and frustration. "Volkov set this whole thing up to take us out."

Olivia nodded grimly. "He's always one step ahead. We need to figure out his source of information."

Jack approached, his face etched with concern. "We lost a lot of good equipment back there," he reported. "And Martinez caught some shrapnel in his leg. He's pretty banged up."

Before Olivia could respond, there was a soft knock at the door; the specific pattern identified their visitor as friendly. Elena moved to open it, revealing Lila, medical bag in hand.

"I came as quickly as I could," Lila said, her eyes sweeping the room. "Who needs attention first?"

As Lila began treating the injuries, Olivia slipped out onto the small balcony, seeking a moment of solitude to collect her thoughts. The cold night air helped clear her head, but it couldn't wash away the guilt she felt at leading her team into such a perilous situation.

She was so lost in thought that she didn't notice Elena joining her until the other woman spoke. "This isn't your fault."

Startled, Olivia turned. "I should have seen it coming. I should have been more cautious."

Elena shook her head. "We all agreed to go in. We knew the risks." She paused, her voice softening slightly. "I'll admit, I had my doubts about your leadership when we first started working together. But after tonight... I've never seen anyone handle a situation like that so well."

Olivia was taken aback by the admission. Though she and Elena had always respected each other professionally, this felt like a deepening of their relationship, forged in the crucible of combat.

"Thanks," Olivia said softly. "That means a lot, especially coming from you." She took a deep breath, steeling herself. "But we need to be smarter, more careful. Volkov is always one step ahead, and that needs to change. We can't let this happen again."

Elena nodded, her eyes glinting with determination. "So, what's our next move?"

Olivia turned back to survey the city, her mind already whirling with their next steps. "We need better intelligence. We need to figure out how Volkov is getting his information, and we need to cut off that supply."

"And operationally?" Elena prompted.

"We tighten everything down," Olivia replied. "No action without triple verification. We can't give Volkov any openings; we change our safe houses, our communication methods, everything."

Elena considered this, then nodded. She turned to face Olivia squarely. "I'm with you," she said, her voice firm. "Whatever it takes, we're bringing Volkov down."

Olivia felt a surge of gratitude and determination. She extended her hand, and Elena grasped it in a firm handshake. In that moment, a new level of trust formed between them—a bond that would be crucial in the challenges to come.

As they rejoined the others, Olivia could see the toll the evening had taken on her team. They were battered emotionally as much as physically. Yet, she felt a swell of pride as she watched each of them: Jack grimly focused on his weapons, Diego hunched over his laptop, already working on improving their security protocols, and the others helping one another as Lila tended to their injuries.

"Listen up, everyone," Olivia called out, her voice cutting through the subdued hum of activity. All eyes turned to her, a mixture of weariness and expectancy.

"Tonight was rough," she began, not sugarcoating the situation. "We walked into a trap and nearly paid the ultimate price for it. But we're still here."

She paused, meeting the gaze of each of her team members. "Volkov thinks he's won. He thinks he's broken us. But he's underestimated us. We're going to use this setback to make ourselves stronger, smarter, better."

As Olivia spoke, she could see a spark of renewed determination igniting in the eyes of her team. "We change everything—our safe houses, our protocols. We leave Volkov no openings, no weaknesses to exploit. We trust no information until it's been verified and re-verified."

She took a deep breath, her voice growing stronger with each word. "It's not going to be easy. The road ahead is going to be hard, maybe the hardest thing we've ever done. But I believe in each and every one of you. Together, we're going to bring Volkov down, whatever it takes."

For a moment, the room was silent as her words sank in. Then, one by one, her team members nodded, their faces set with fresh resolve.

Jack spoke up, voicing what they all felt: "We're with you, Olivia. All the way."

Olivia felt a surge of hope as she looked around at her team: battered but unbroken, determined to see their mission through to the end.

Chapter 13: Chase from the Caribbean

Olivia Raines walked deliberately toward the command center as the Caribbean sun hammered fiercely on the Coast Guard cutter Sentinel's deck. The weight of expectation and the promise of peril carried with the salty wind that blew across her hair. Today was the day they had been waiting for—the day they would at last get a chance to catch Andrei Volkov and his illegal weapons delivery.

Olivia's squad welcomed her with concentrated expressions as she approached the command center. Their intelligence expert, Elena Salazar, was already bent over a bank of monitors, her fingers speeding over the keyboard as she retrieved the most recent satellite pictures. Nearby, Jack Tanner and Natalie Harper were deep in conversation about the equipment improvements they had been working on. Diego Ortega sat in the corner, carefully reading over a comprehensive Caribbean map, his forehead wrinkled in concentration.

"Alright, team," Olivia said, her voice slicing through the buzz of activity. "We have strong intelligence that Volkov is on the move. This could be our best—and maybe only—chance to find him and stop his operation. Let's get up to speed."

As Elena pulled up a high-resolution map of the Caribbean, the crew gathered around the center console. "Our satellite imagery suggests Volkov's vessel will be taking this route," she continued, tracing a line that snaked over several important sites in the area. "He's definitely trying to avoid known patrol areas and the main shipping lanes."

Olivia nodded as her eyes followed the expected trajectory. "Good work, Elena. Diego, what can you tell us about the terrain?"

Diego moved forward, the fire of his experience ablaze in his eyes. "Volkov's selected a difficult path," he said, pointing to several places on the map. "These clusters of little islands and hidden coves could provide excellent cover. If he's as well-informed as we think he is, he'll know about these shortcuts and hiding places. We'll need to be prepared for sudden course changes and evasive maneuvers."

"Understood," Olivia said, her head already whirling with several approaches. "Jack, Natalie, how are we looking on tools?"

Jack straightened, a hint of pride in his voice. "We should be able to maintain contact even if Volkov tries to jam our signals. Natalie's also rigged some new toys for our boarding party—state-of-the-art, virtually undetectable. We've improved the Sentinel's tracking and communication systems."

Natalie nodded in agreement. "Captain, we're as ready as we can ever be."

Breathing deeply, Olivia stared each member of her team in the eye. "Alright, people. Jack, you'll be leading the tactical unit. Be ready for a possible boarding action at a moment's notice. Elena, I want you on comms and satellite tracking—every piece of information could be crucial. Diego, you'll be our navigator; your knowledge of these waters could give us the edge we need. Natalie's on weapons and defense systems; keep us in the fight if things get hot."

Olivia felt a flash of satisfaction as her staff nodded with comprehension. Selected for this purpose, they were the finest of the best. If anyone could bring down Volkov, it was them.

Her voice low and fierce, she said, "Remember, Volkov is dangerous and desperate. He knows we're closing in, and he'll do anything to complete this shipment. Stay sharp, trust your training, and above all, watch each other's backs. Let's move out."

The crew dispersed to their stations, affirming their readiness. Olivia headed for the bridge, her gait on the metal deck resonant with intent. She could feel the Sentinel's eagerness to start the pursuit thrumming under her feet as she positioned herself at the helm.

Over the intercom, she said, "All stations, report in."

Her staff verified their preparedness one by one. Olivia pushed the throttle forward, casting one last glance at the pure blue horizon. The Sentinel raced forward, cutting over the waves with determination as they set out in search of their prey.

Following Elena's intelligence path, the Sentinel pounded across the Caribbean for hours. Every crew member on board was visibly tense, always aware that Volkov's vessel was just beyond the horizon.

The first complication arose as they were crossing a tight strait between two small, deserted islands. The radio buzzed to life, a familiar but unwelcome voice filling the bridge.

"Sentinel, come in. This is Captain Maxwell Thorne of the Defender. Over."

Olivia grabbed for the radio, setting her jaw. "This is Captain Raines. What can we do for you, Captain Thorne?"

Thorne's voice dripped with barely veiled contempt. "I'm assuming control of this operation. You will fall in behind the Defender and follow my lead. We have actionable intelligence on Volkov's whereabouts and will be proceeding with the interception."

Olivia was momentarily struck silent with shock. She turned to see Elena shaking her head fiercely. There was no chance Thorne's information was better than theirs.

"Negative, Captain Thorne," Olivia said, striving to keep her voice steady. "We are proceeding on our current course based on confirmed intelligence. Your assistance is not required at this time."

There was a pause, and when Thorne's voice returned, it was sharp with anger. "This is not a request, Captain Raines. Fall in line, or I'll have you up on charges of insubordination."

Olivia gripped the radio, her knuckles turning white. "Captain Thorne, with all due respect, this is our operation. We have been tracking Volkov for months, and we are not about to jeopardize this mission based on your unverified claims. Stand down and return to your patrol path."

Thorne's angry response blasted over the radio, but Olivia had already switched him off. Her eyes blazing with determination, she turned to face her crew. "Maintain course and speed. Elena, monitor the Defender's movements. Jack, be ready for any attempts at interference."

The Defender appeared off their starboard side, matching their pace as if on cue. Olivia could see Thorne on the bridge, his face a mask of rage as he gestured broadly.

"He's deploying boarding craft!" Natalie called out, her eyes fixed on the radar panel.

Olivia's thoughts raced. Thorne was essentially attempting to seize command of their mission through coercion. It was a shockingly bold move.

"Evasive maneuvers," she ordered, her voice cool despite her tension. "Diego, find us a route that will slow them down without taking us off course."

Diego's hands flew over the navigation controls, and the Sentinel banked sharply to port, weaving through a series of rocky outcrops. Larger and less agile, the Defender fell behind, its boarding boats struggling to keep up in the choppy waves.

"Nice work, Diego," Olivia said, allowing herself a small smile. "That should buy us some time. Elena, any sign of Volkov?"

Elena shook her head, frustration evident in her voice. "Nothing yet, Captain. But if we stay on this course, we should be reaching his anticipated position within the hour."

Olivia nodded, her mind already moving beyond the distraction Thorne had created. "Alright, people. Stay focused. Thorne's interference has cost us time, but we're still in this. Keep your eyes peeled and your minds sharp. Volkov's out there, and we will find him."

As the Sentinel pressed on, leaving the irate Captain Thorne in their wake, Olivia couldn't shake the feeling that their troubles were just beginning. Volkov was cunning, and Thorne's unexpected intervention had raised the stakes. However, as she surveyed her determined team, she knew they were ready for whatever challenges lay ahead.

The next hour passed in tense silence, broken only occasionally by crew status updates. The Caribbean sun had begun its descent toward the horizon, painting the sky in stunning hues of orange and pink. But the crew of the Sentinel missed the beauty of the sunset as their instruments scanned the seas for any sign of their target.

Suddenly, Natalie's voice cut through the silence. "Contact! Bearing 030, distance 12 nautical miles! Profile match for Volkov's vessel!"

The air on the bridge instantly charged with electricity. Olivia leaned forward, eyes fixed on the radar screen. "Are you certain it's him, Natalie?"

Natalie's fingers flew across her console. "As sure as I can be, Captain," she replied. "The size, speed, and emission signature all match our intel."

Olivia nodded, her decision instantaneous. "Okay, this is it. Jack, get your boarding team ready. Elena, start tracking any communications. Diego, plot an intercept course."

Olivia felt the familiar surge of adrenaline as her orders were executed. This was what they had been waiting for, training for. Everything hinged on the next few minutes.

"Engaging pursuit speed," she called out, pushing the Sentinel's engines to their limit. The ship surged forward, eating up the distance between them and their quarry.

As they drew closer, Olivia could make out the sleek form of Volkov's vessel through her binoculars. It was a custom-built speedboat, designed for both speed and stealth. Even as she watched, she saw a flurry of activity on its deck. They'd been spotted.

"They're making a run for it!" Diego shouted, his eyes on the navigation screens. "They're heading for that cluster of islands to the northeast."

Olivia clenched her jaw. It was a smart move, one they'd anticipated. Volkov was trying to lose them in the maze-like channels between the islands.

"Stay on them," she ordered. "Diego, use your knowledge of these waters to find us a shortcut."

What followed was a high-stakes game of cat and mouse through the island chain. Volkov's ship zipped between narrow gaps, its superior speed widening the distance. But Olivia's skilled helmsmanship and Diego's expert navigation kept the Sentinel hot on its trail.

"Captain," Elena called out, her voice tense with excitement, "I'm picking up a transmission from Volkov's ship. It's encrypted, but I'm working on it now."

"Good work," Olivia said, her eyes never leaving the fleeing ship. "Let me know as soon as you have anything."

The chase continued, the two ships engaged in a deadly dance across the island chain. Several times Volkov's ship seemed to vanish, only for Diego to anticipate its trajectory and guide the Sentinel back into pursuit.

After what felt like hours but was really only forty minutes, Elena's voice rang out again. "Captain, you need to hear this! I've cracked the encryption."

Olivia nodded, and Elena played the decoded audio over the bridge speakers. A tense, accented male voice filled the air.

"...must reach the drop point by nightfall; the buyers will only wait so long. If we miss this window, the entire operation is compromised. Push the engines if you have to, but get us to Santo Porto. The dock master there has been paid off and will ensure we can offload without interference."

The transmission cut off, leaving the bridge in a moment of stunned silence. The implications of what they had just heard raced through Olivia's mind.

"Santo Porto," she said aloud. "It's a small port, but it's close to one of the busiest shipping lanes in the Caribbean. Once those weapons are offloaded and mixed in with legitimate cargo..."

"They'll be almost impossible to track," Jack finished, his expression grim.

Olivia nodded, her resolve hardening. "We can't let that happen. Diego, how far are we from Santo Porto?"

Diego consulted his charts. "At our current speed, about an hour. Volkov's ship is faster; they'll beat us there by at least twenty minutes."

"Not good enough," Olivia muttered. She studied the navigation display, an idea forming. "Diego, what about that passage there?" She pointed to a narrow waterway between two islands.

Diego's eyes widened. "It's dangerous, Captain. The channel's narrow and full of hidden shoals. One wrong move and we'll run aground."

"But it would cut off a good chunk of Volkov's lead?"

Diego nodded reluctantly. "If we could make it through... yes, it would put us right on their tail as they approach Santo Porto."

Olivia didn't hesitate. "Then that's our play. All hands, brace for high-speed maneuvering. Diego, take the helm. If anyone can get us through that channel, it's you."

As Diego took control, Olivia turned to address her crew. "This is going to be close. Jack, have your boarding team ready to move the instant we're in range. Natalie, be prepared to disable Volkov's engines if we can't board. Elena, alert the Santo Porto authorities. Tell them to lock down the port, but keep it quiet. We don't want to spook Volkov before we can get to him."

The crew sprang into action with a chorus of affirmatives. Olivia felt the Sentinel heel over as Diego guided them into the treacherous passage. Sharp rocks loomed menacingly on either side as the ship bucked and shuddered through the narrow waterway.

Olivia gripped the railing with white knuckles as Diego navigated the dangerous waters with near-magical skill. Twice they came so close to the rocks she could have reached out and touched them. But each time, Diego made a minute adjustment, guiding the Sentinel through with razor-sharp control.

Several heart-stopping minutes later, they emerged from the channel into open water. And there, just ahead of them, was Volkov's ship.

"All ahead full!" Olivia shouted. "Natalie, target their engines. Jack, ready to board!"

The Sentinel surged forward, rapidly closing the gap to Volkov's vessel. Olivia could see figures scrambling on the other ship's deck, clearly taken by surprise at the Sentinel's sudden appearance.

"They're powering up weapons!" Natalie called out.

"Evasive maneuvers!" Olivia ordered. "Return fire, targeting weapons only. We need that ship intact!"

The air filled with gunfire as the two ships exchanged salvos. The Sentinel shuddered as a shot from Volkov's ship grazed her hull, but Natalie's more precise return fire disabled one of the enemy vessel's weapon emplacements.

"We're in boarding range!" Jack yelled over the din.

Olivia nodded grimly. "Do it!"

Jack and his team launched from the Sentinel in a well-practiced maneuver, grappling hooks arcing across the narrowing gap between the ships. Volkov's crew fired heavily, but Jack's team managed to gain a foothold on the enemy vessel.

"Suppressing fire!" Olivia commanded, and Natalie complied, laying down a barrage that forced Volkov's men to take cover, giving Jack's team the opportunity to fully board.

From her vantage point on the Sentinel's bridge, Olivia could only watch as a brutal close-quarters fight raged aboard Volkov's ship. Jack and his team moved like a well-oiled machine, covering each other as they methodically neutralized the resistance.

"Captain!" Elena's voice cut through the chaos. "I have a visual on Volkov! He's making

to the bridge!"

Olivia's eyes widened to see the tall, silver-haired guy Elena had pointed across the deck dodging and whirling through the battle.

Olivia grabbed a gun without thinking and headed toward the boarding lines. "Elena, you have the Conn. Keep us steady!"

Ignoring her crew's cries of protest, Olivia shot herself over the distance between the ships. She slammed the Volkov's deck hard, rolling to absorb the force then sprung to her feet.

All around her, the struggle raged. Jack and his squad were in advantage, but Volkov's troops were battling with the ferocity of trapped animals.

Chapter 14: Dilemma of the Informant

"Ms. Raines," a voice called from across the room. Olivia looked up to see Diego approaching, accompanied by two of her security personnel. "I wanted to thank you. For everything you're doing for my family."

Olivia regarded him briefly before responding. "You realize, Mr. Ortega, the road ahead won't be easy. This is only the beginning."

Diego nodded solemnly. "I know, but it's worth it to keep them safe and to finally do the right thing."

Before Olivia could reply, a thunderous explosion rocked the building. Alarms blared as smoke began to fill the room. In an instant, the relative calm of the operations center dissolved into chaos.

"We're under attack!" Jack Tanner's voice shouted over the tumult. "Volkov's men have breached the perimeter!"

Olivia's training kicked in immediately. "Defensive positions!" she commanded, her voice cutting through the pandemonium. "Natalie, secure our systems and alert backup. Elena—with me. We need to repel this assault."

As her team rushed to respond, Olivia turned to Diego. "This is your chance to prove your loyalty, Ortega. Are you with us?"

Diego's face was pale, but his jaw was set with determination. "I'm with you. Tell me what to do."

Olivia handed him a sidearm. "Stay close and watch our backs. This is going to get messy."

The next few minutes were a blur of explosions and gunfire. Led by Olivia, her team navigated their defense against Volkov's agents through the safe house. Although the attackers were well-trained and heavily armed, Olivia's side had the advantage of home territory and a fierce determination to protect their own.

Jack Tanner provided covering fire for the rest of the team, moving with the precision of his military training, each shot finding its mark. Elena Salazar was a whirlwind of motion, her hand-to-hand combat skills proving invaluable in the tight confines of the safe house corridors.

To Olivia's surprise, Diego Ortega proved to be a capable fighter. His knowledge of Volkov's tactics helped him anticipate the attackers' moves, allowing him to provide crucial warnings and information as they fought to stem the assault.

As they drove the assailants back toward the perimeter, Olivia caught sight of a familiar face: Viktor Dragovic, Alexei Volkov's right-hand man. He was directing the attack, barking orders to his men as they attempted to penetrate the inner sanctum of the safe house.

"Dragovic!" Olivia shouted, her voice carrying over the cacophony of battle. "You can't win this! It's over!"

Viktor turned, his gaze locking onto Olivia with a mixture of contempt and grudging respect. "You've gotten sloppy, Raines!" he shouted back. "Volkov sends his regards! Letting a rat like Ortega into your midst!"

Viktor then signaled to his remaining men, and they began a fighting retreat. Olivia and her team pressed their advantage, driving the attackers back and out of the compound. As the last of Volkov's soldiers disappeared into the darkness, Olivia allowed herself to relax slightly.

"Secure the perimeter," she ordered, her voice hoarse from shouting. "I want a full sweep of the compound. Make sure there are no surprises left behind."

As her team moved to obey her commands, Olivia turned to find Diego Ortega standing nearby, his face streaked with soot and wearing a grim expression of determination.

"I hope that was sufficient proof of my loyalty," he said quietly.

Olivia regarded him for a long moment before nodding. "It's a start," she said. "But we need to regroup and decide our next move. We're not out of the woods yet."

As they made their way back to the operations center, Olivia's mind was racing. The attack confirmed Volkov's knowledge of Diego's defection, thus validating the authenticity of the information he had provided. It also meant, however, that their adversary was more desperate and more dangerous than ever before.

The operations center was a hive of activity as Olivia and her team reassembled. Natalie Harper was diligently restoring their systems and investigating any potential data breaches. Jack Tanner and Elena Salazar were coordinating with the backup teams that had responded to their distress call, ensuring the compound was truly secure.

"Status report," Olivia called out as she entered the room.

"Perimeter is secure," Jack reported. "We have teams sweeping the surrounding area, but it looks like Volkov's men have completely withdrawn."

Elena stepped forward, holding a tablet. "We have three wounded, nothing life-threatening. Medical team is treating them now."

Natalie looked up from her bank of computers. "Systems are coming back online. No sign of data breaches, but I'm running a full diagnostic to be sure."

Olivia nodded, processing the information. "Good work, everyone. Volkov knows we have his intel, which means our window of opportunity is closing fast. Now we have to decide what to do with it."

She turned to Diego, who stood silently at the periphery of the group. "Mr. Ortega, it's time to put your information to the test. We need to move on that weapons shipment, and we need to do it now."

Diego nodded and stepped forward to join the team gathered around the central planning table. As he began to delve into the specifics of Volkov's plan, Olivia felt a sense of resolve settle over her. They had weathered the storm; now it was time to strike back.

For the next hour, the team worked feverishly over maps and satellite imagery, formulating a strategy to intercept Volkov's weapons shipment. Jack Tanner proposed a multi-pronged approach where small teams would simultaneously target key nodes along the smuggling route.

"If we coordinate with local law enforcement," Jack said, indicating several points on the map, "we can set up choke points here, here, and here. Cut off their escape routes and force them into a trap."

Elena nodded in agreement. "And if we time it right, we can catch Volkov's key lieutenants in the act. That kind of evidence would be impossible to ignore, even for his bought-and-paid-for friends in high places."

Olivia felt a growing sense of excitement as the plan took shape. This was the opportunity they had been waiting for—a chance to deliver a crippling blow to Volkov's entire operation.

"Alright," she said, looking around at her team. "We move in 36 hours. I want every detail of this operation locked down. Natalie, you'll coordinate communications from here. Jack, Elena—you'll lead the ground teams. And Diego, your knowledge of Volkov's operation could be crucial in the field."

Diego nodded, his face showing a mixture of anxiety and determination. "I'm ready. Whatever it takes to bring Volkov down."

As the team dispersed to finalize preparations, Olivia paused. She turned to see the first hints of dawn peeking over the horizon. The next thirty-six hours would define everything: the fate of their mission, the future of countless individuals affected by Volkov's criminal empire, and perhaps even her own destiny.

She thought back to the beginning of this journey, to the moment she had first vowed to bring down Alexei Volkov. Back then, it had seemed like an impossibility, a battle against a shadow that was always one step ahead. But now, poised on the brink of what could be their defining moment, Olivia felt a surge of confidence.

They had endured brutality, treachery, and seemingly insurmountable odds. Yet here they stood, battered but unbroken, ready to strike at the heart of Volkov's operation. Olivia allowed herself a small smile. Whatever the outcome, she knew that every sacrifice, every sleepless night, every hard-won piece of intelligence had led to this moment.

As the sun continued its ascent, bathing the operations center in a warm glow, Olivia straightened her shoulders and turned back to her team. There was work to be done, a meticulous dance of planning and preparation that would determine their success or failure.

"Alright, people," she called out, her voice steady and resolute. "Let's run through it again. I want to know every possible scenario, every potential hiccup. We're not leaving anything to chance."

The room buzzed with renewed energy as her team dove back into their tasks. Natalie's fingers flew over her keyboard, setting up secure communication channels and running final checks on their systems. Jack and Elena huddled over tactical maps, fine-tuning their approach vectors and discussing contingency plans.

In the midst of it all, Diego sat at a corner desk, poring over documents and occasionally conferring with other team members. His presence was a constant reminder of the high stakes they were playing for—not just the success of their mission, but the lives of his family and countless others affected by Volkov's reign of terror.

As the hours ticked by, Olivia felt a familiar tension building in her muscles, a coiled energy born of anticipation and determination. She moved from station to station, reviewing plans, offering suggestions, and ensuring that every team member was prepared for what lay ahead.

By the time the sun had completed its arc across the sky and darkness once again enveloped the safe house, their plan had taken on a life of its own. It was a complex web of coordinated actions, each piece carefully designed to neutralize Volkov's operation and bring his key players to justice.

Olivia gathered her core team for a final briefing. As she looked around at the determined faces of Jack, Elena, Natalie, and Diego, she felt a swell of pride. These individuals, each carrying their own burdens and motivations, had come together to fight for something greater than themselves.

"In a few hours, we'll be setting this plan in motion," Olivia began, her voice calm but charged with purpose. "I won't sugarcoat it—this is going to be dangerous. Volkov and his people will fight back with everything they've got. But remember why we're doing this. Remember all the lives that have been destroyed by his greed and cruelty. Remember that we might be the only ones who can stop him."

She paused, making eye contact with each team member. "I have faith in each of you, and in the plan we've crafted together. Stay focused, watch each other's backs, and remember your training. If we pull this off, we'll be dealing a blow to organized crime that will be felt for years to come."

As the meeting concluded and her team moved to make their final preparations, Olivia found herself alone in the operations center. She stood before the large screen displaying their battle plan, each point of attack highlighted in glowing red.

For a moment, she allowed herself to imagine success—Volkov in handcuffs, his network in shambles, justice finally served for all those who had suffered under his reign. But she quickly pushed the thought aside. There would be time for celebration later, if they succeeded. For now, she needed to focus on the task at hand.

Olivia took a deep breath, centering herself. As she exhaled, she felt the last vestiges of doubt and uncertainty leave her body. In their place was a steely resolve, a determination that had been forged through years of struggle and sacrifice.

She glanced at her watch. It was time. With a final look at the battle plan, Olivia turned and strode purposefully toward the door. The next few hours would determine everything, and she was ready to face whatever challenges lay ahead.

As she joined her team in the staging area, Olivia felt a sense of calm settle over her. They had prepared for this moment, had accounted for every variable they could think of. Now, it was time to put their plan into action and bring Alexei Volkov's empire crumbling down.

With a nod to her team, Olivia gave the signal. "Operation Checkmate is a go. Good luck, everyone. Let's make this count."

And with that, they moved out into the night, ready to face their destiny and change the course of history.

Chapter 15: Revealing Betrayal

Olivia Raines, Jack Tanner, and Elena Salazar gathered around the central console, the command center humming with anxiety. Weeks of intense observation and study had led to this moment. As they reviewed the final pieces of data meant to expose the traitor among them, the air seemed heavy with expectation.

Olivia's thoughts raced to absorb the information before her. Her eyes flicked over the displays. For some time, she had suspected a mole; nevertheless, nothing could have prepared her for the reality about to shatter her world.

"It can't be," she whispered, her voice barely audible above the low hum of the machinery.

Jack leaned in, his brow furrowed. "Olivia, are you certain about this?"

Her chest tightened as the realization struck. She nodded slowly. "Sarah. Lieutenant Collins is our mole."

The name lingered there like a thunderclap. Olivia's long-time friend and confidante, Sarah Collins, had been providing information to the enemy. The treachery cut deep, threatening to tear apart the very foundation of their team's cohesion.

Elena's hand rested on Olivia's shoulder, offering silent support amid this terrible disclosure. "We have to move fast," she remarked, her voice cool but firm. "Sarah might compromise the whole operation if she discovers we're onto her."

Olivia inhaled deeply, forcing herself to compartmentalize her emotions. With so much at stake, she couldn't allow her feelings to cloud her judgment. "You're right," she said, straightening. "Jack, you and Elena should prepare for Sarah's detention. We can't afford any mistakes and need all the evidence in order."

Jack nodded, his face grim. "Understood. What about you?"

"I'll handle Sarah personally," Olivia said, her voice firm despite the turmoil within her. "She trusts me. I'll bring her in under the pretext of a routine briefing. Once we're alone, I'll confront her with what we know."

As Jack and Elena set about their tasks, Olivia steeled herself for what was to come. Throughout her career, she had faced numerous perilous situations, but none had seemed as daunting as the one that lay ahead.

Olivia strode through the corridors of their base with measured steps. She found Sarah in the communications room, working on satellite imagery. For a moment, Olivia observed her friend at work, searching for any sign of the deceit that had been hidden for so long.

"Sarah," Olivia called out, keeping her voice neutral. "I need you for a briefing. Something's come up."

Sarah looked up, her expression one of mild curiosity. "Of course, Liv. Lead the way."

As they walked side by side to a private conference room, Olivia mourned the friendship about to be lost. There was no turning back; years of shared experiences, laughter, and trust were about to crumble.

Once inside, Olivia gestured for Sarah to sit. The door closed softly behind them. "Thanks for coming on such short notice," she said, her tone deliberately casual.

Sarah leaned back in her chair. "No problem. What's this about?"

Olivia remained standing, hands clasped behind her back. She took a deep breath, then fixed Sarah with an unwavering gaze. "It's about you, Sarah. About what you've been doing behind our backs."

Sarah's expression shifted subtly but unmistakably. A flicker of fear crossed her face before she regained control. "I'm not sure I understand," she said, her voice carefully modulated.

"I think you do," Olivia replied, her tone hardening. She reached for a tablet on the nearby table and began swiping through files. "We have evidence of multiple information leaks over the past six months. Classified intelligence finding its way into the hands of Volkov's syndicate. Missions compromised before they even began."

Sarah paled but maintained her composure. "Olivia, you can't possibly think—"

"It's not what I think," Olivia cut her off sharply. "It's what I know." She turned the tablet toward Sarah, displaying a series of damning records and surveillance photos. "We know you're the mole. We have financial records, communications logs, even footage of you meeting known Volkov operatives. It's over, Sarah."

The facade crumbled. Sarah's shoulders slumped, and she buried her face in her hands. When she looked up again, her eyes were brimming with tears. "Liv, please, you have to understand. I had no choice. They threatened my family."

Olivia felt a surge of disappointment and anger. "There's always a choice, Sarah. You could have come to me. We could have protected your family, found another way. Instead, you betrayed everything we stand for. People have died because of the information you leaked."

Sarah flinched at the accusation but didn't deny it. "I know," she whispered. "And I'll have to live with that for the rest of my life. But you have to believe me, Liv. Volkov's people are monsters. They showed me pictures of my parents' house, my sister's kids at school. They said they would kill them all if I didn't cooperate."

Olivia paced the room, trying to reconcile the woman before her with the friend she thought she knew. "How long?" she demanded. "How long have you been working for them?"

"Eight months," Sarah said, her voice barely audible. "It started small. Just bits of information here and there. But they kept demanding more, and I... I couldn't see a way out."

The admission hit Olivia like a physical blow. Eight months of lies, endangering the entire team. She leaned against the wall, feeling the weight of every sleepless night and close call they had endured.

"I want names," Olivia said at last, her voice cold. "Contacts, meeting locations, everything you know about Volkov's operation. If you have any hope of salvaging anything from this mess, you'll give me everything."

Sarah nodded, her eyes gleaming with a faint glimmer of hope. "I will. I'll tell you everything I know. Maybe... maybe it will help make things right."

Over the next hour, Sarah poured out a torrent of information. She detailed her handlers, the communication methods they used, and key aspects of Volkov's network she had become privy to. Olivia listened intently, her mind already processing how this new intelligence could be leveraged against the syndicate.

As Sarah's confession drew to a close, Olivia stood. "You'll be placed under guard," she told her former friend. "We'll verify everything you've told us. If it proves accurate, it could help your case when this goes to trial."

Sarah nodded, accepting her fate. "I understand. And Liv... I'm sorry. For everything."

Olivia paused at the door, her hand on the handle. Without turning back, she spoke, her voice thick with emotion. "So am I, Sarah. So am I."

As she left the room, Olivia found Jack and Elena waiting. She nodded, signaling for them to take Sarah into custody. Watching them lead her away, Olivia felt a complex mixture of anger, grief, and determination.

There was no time to dwell on personal betrayals, however. Sarah had provided information that required immediate action. Olivia headed back to the command center, her mind already shifting focus to the broader mission.

Lost in thought, she almost missed Natalie Harper's sharp wave from across the room. "Olivia," Natalie called, her voice tense. "You need to see this. Now."

Frowning, Olivia approached Natalie's workstation. "What is it?"

Natalie's fingers flew across her keyboard, pulling up a series of financial documents. "Based on Sarah's intel, I was digging deeper into Volkov's financial network, but I found something... something I don't think even she knew about."

Olivia leaned in, scanning the documents on the screen. At first, the columns of transaction logs and figures seemed unremarkable. Then, her blood ran cold as she spotted a familiar name.

"No," she breathed, her fingers gripping the edge of the desk. "This can't be right."

But the evidence was there in black and white. Large transactions from shell companies linked to Volkov's syndicate, all funneling to one recipient: Senator Richard Raines. Her father.

Olivia felt as if the ground had dropped out from beneath her feet. First Sarah, and now this. The day seemed intent on revelations, each one cutting deeper than the last.

Elena approached, concern etched on her face. "Olivia? What's wrong?"

Olivia gestured silently toward the screen. As Elena absorbed the information, her eyes widened. "Dios mío," she murmured. "Your father?"

Olivia nodded, her mind reeling. "We have to handle this delicately," Elena said, her voice low. "If word gets out that a sitting senator has ties to Volkov's syndicate..."

"It would be a political earthquake," Olivia finished. She straightened, her jaw set with determination. "I need to speak with him personally."

Elena looked uncertain. "Are you sure that's wise? Perhaps we should gather more evidence first, build a stronger case."

Olivia shook her head. "No," she said softly. "I need to hear it from him. I need to understand why."

Elena nodded, recognizing the resolve in Olivia's voice. "Alright. But be careful. This is personal now, not just about the mission."

Olivia managed a grim smile. "It's been personal from the start, Elena. I just didn't know how deep it went."

Within the hour, Olivia had arranged a meeting with her father. Unaware that his daughter now knew the extent of his wrongdoing, Senator Richard Raines arrived at the secure location. As Olivia watched him approach through the conference room's glass walls, she felt a conflicting mix of emotions: anger, disappointment, and a desperate hope that some explanation might salvage their relationship.

"Olivia," Senator Raines greeted her warmly as he entered, moving to embrace her. "This is an unexpected pleasure. Your message sounded urgent. Is everything alright?"

Olivia stepped back, avoiding the embrace. The gesture, once comforting, now felt like another lie. "Sit down, Dad," she said, her voice controlled. "We need to talk."

The Senator's face flickered with uncertainty, but he complied, taking a seat across from her. "You're worrying me, sweetheart. What's this about?"

Olivia took a deep breath, then placed a folder between them on the table. "It's about this," she said, opening it to reveal Natalie's uncovered financial records. "It's about your connection to Anton Volkov and his crime syndicate."

Senator Raines's face drained of color. For a moment, he seemed at a loss for words. Then his political instincts kicked in. "Olivia, I'm not sure where you obtained this information, but I can assure you it's taken out of context. These are all legitimate international investments, part of a series of—"

"Stop," Olivia cut him off, her voice sharp. "Don't lie to me, Dad. Not now. We have records of meetings, of favors exchanged. I know everything. We've traced these shell companies directly to Volkov's organization."

The Senator's shoulders sagged, the fight leaving him. He suddenly looked older, more tired. "How long have you known?" he asked quietly.

"Long enough," Olivia replied. "What I don't know is why. Was it just about the money? Or was there more? How could you get involved with someone like Volkov?"

Senator Raines ran a hand through his graying hair, a gesture of frustration Olivia had seen many times growing up. "It didn't start out this way," he said, his voice thick with regret. "The money was good, and I told myself I was helping to bridge gaps between Eastern Europe and the West. But Volkov... he's not a man you can simply walk away from once you're in his orbit."

Olivia leaned forward, her eyes locked on her father's. "So you just went along with it? Turned a blind eye to the lives he's ruined, the people he's killed?"

"I tried to mitigate the damage," the Senator said softly. "Used my position to steer things away from the worst excesses. But yes, I became complicit. And with each compromise, it became harder to see a way out."

The admission hung between them. Olivia felt a swirl of complex emotions: anger at her father's weakness, sympathy for the trap he'd found himself in, and an overwhelming, aching grief for the death of the man she thought she knew.

"Do you have any idea?" she said slowly, struggling to keep her voice steady. "The danger you've put my team in? People have died, Dad. Good people."

The Senator's face crumpled. "You have to believe me, Olivia. I love you. I would never knowingly put you in danger. I never meant for any of this to happen."

"But you did," Olivia said. "Every time you fed information to Volkov, every time you used your influence to help his organization, you put me and my team at risk. How am I supposed to trust anything you say now?"

Father and daughter stared at each other across the table, a long silence stretching between them. Finally, Senator Raines spoke, his voice barely above a whisper. "What happens now?"

Olivia leaned back, considering. Part of her wanted to call in her team, have her father arrested on the spot. But another part, the one that still remembered bedtime stories and proud smiles at her academy graduation, hesitated.

"That depends on you," she said at last. "Every contact, every piece of information you have on Volkov's operation. If you help us bring him down, maybe – maybe – we can work out some kind of deal to mitigate the consequences."

Hope flickered in the Senator's eyes. "You'd do that? After everything?"

"I'm not making any promises," Olivia cautioned. "But if your information proves valuable enough, if it helps us dismantle Volkov's network... it could make a difference."

Senator Raines nodded eagerly. "Anything you need. I'll tell you everything I know."

Over the next few hours, Olivia listened as her father detailed the extent of his involvement with Volkov's syndicate. She took careful notes, her training helping her to separate her personal emotions from her focus on the intelligence being provided.

As the debriefing concluded, Olivia stood. "My team will verify everything you've told me," she said, her voice businesslike. "For now, you'll be placed in protective custody. To ensure you remain available for further questions, and for your own safety."

The Senator nodded, understanding the unspoken implication. He was, for all intents and purposes, under arrest. "Olivia," he said softly as she turned to leave. "I am sorry. Truly. I know it doesn't change anything, but—"

Olivia paused at the door, her hand on the handle. Without turning back, she spoke, her voice thick with emotion. "No, Dad. It doesn't. I learned from you that actions have consequences. Now it's time for you to face yours."

She left the room, signaling for the waiting security team to take her father into custody. As they led him away, Olivia leaned against the wall, suddenly feeling the weight of the day's revelations crashing down on her.

But there was no time to dwell on personal turmoil. The information provided by Sarah and her father had opened up new avenues in their quest against Volkov. It was time to regroup, refocus, and plan their next move.

Olivia returned to the command center, where she found her team already assembled. Jack, Elena, Natalie, and Diego turned to face her, their expressions a mix of concern and resolve.

"Alright, people," Olivia said, her voice steady despite the emotional upheaval of the past several hours. "We have some significant developments. I know the revelations about Sarah and my father have shocked all of us. Right now, we need to set personal feelings aside and focus on the mission."

She moved to the central console and brought up a series of maps and data points. "Thanks to the information we've gathered, we now have unprecedented insight into Volkov's operations. Elena, can you summarize what we're looking at?"

Elena stepped forward, her fingers dancing over the touchpad. "Volkov's network is more extensive than we initially thought," she said. "We've identified multiple front businesses used for money laundering and arms deals across six different countries, as well as key financial hubs."

She zoomed in on a map of Eastern Europe, highlighting several locations. "These are the primary bases of operation we've confirmed. The political protection Volkov has been enjoying has been particularly facilitated by Senator Raines's intelligence."

Jack Tanner leaned in, studying the map intently. "With this knowledge, we could potentially disrupt their entire financial structure," he said. "Hit them where it really hurts."

Olivia nodded, a grim smile playing at her lips. "Exactly. Diego, based on what we've learned, what can you tell us about their financial activities?"

Diego Ortega pulled up a series of complex graphs. "It's a sophisticated system," he said. "Now that we know the structure, we can start to unravel it. They're moving money through a combination of cryptocurrency exchanges, shell companies, and old-fashioned bribery."

"Good," Olivia said. "Work with our contacts in international financial institutions. We need to cut off their cash flow. I want a plan to freeze their assets and expose their illegal activities."

As Diego nodded and began furiously typing on his tablet, Olivia turned to Natalie. "What about our surveillance capabilities? Can we enhance our monitoring based on the new intelligence?"

Natalie Harper's eyes lit up with excitement. "Absolutely. Now that we know their communication protocols, I can fine-tune our systems to intercept and decode their messages in real-time. We'll have eyes and ears on every major player in Volkov's organization."

"Excellent," Olivia said. "I want constant updates. If Volkov so much as sneezes, I want to know about it."

She paused, looking around at her team. Despite the betrayals they'd endured and the personal cost to her, Olivia felt a surge of pride in the professionals surrounding her. They had weathered the storm and emerged stronger, more determined than ever.

"Listen up, everyone," she said, her voice carrying the weight of authority. "What we've learned today changes everything. We have a unique opportunity to deal a crippling blow to Volkov's syndicate. But it also means we're more vulnerable than ever. Desperate criminals are the most dangerous kind."

Jack stepped forward, his face grim. "We should assume Volkov knows we're onto him. Sarah's and the Senator's information might be compromised. We need to move fast."

Elena nodded in agreement. "I've already contacted our allied agencies. We have support ready to move on our signal at key locations."

Olivia felt a surge of resolve. This was what they had been working towards for so long. Despite the emotional toll and personal betrayals, they were closer than ever to dismantling one of the most dangerous criminal organizations in the world.

"Alright, here's how we're going to play this," she said, outlining their strategy. "Diego, I want you working with our financial task force. Start freezing assets and tracking money flows. Jack, coordinate with Elena on the ground teams. We'll need synchronized raids on multiple locations."

She turned to Natalie. "I need you to be our eyes and ears. Track movements. If Volkov tries to slip away, I want to know where he's headed before he does."

As her team sprang into action, each member focused on their task with renewed energy, Olivia allowed herself a moment of introspection. The past few hours had shaken her to her core, making her question relationships she had always taken for granted. But it had also reinforced the bonds she shared with her team.

They were here, ready to follow her into the fire, having seen her at her most vulnerable and witnessed her personal life unravel. It was a sobering realization, one that motivated her even more to see their mission through to its end.

As the command center buzzed with activity, Olivia moved from station to station, checking plans, offering guidance, and ensuring every aspect of their operation was flawless. They couldn't afford any missteps, not when they were so close to their goal.

Hours passed in a blur of tactical discussions, intelligence analysis, and coordination with international partners. As the pieces of their plan fell into place, Olivia felt a growing sense of anticipation. They were about to embark on something monumental, an operation that could potentially dismantle one of the most pervasive criminal networks in recent history.

As the deadline for action approached, Olivia gathered her team for a final briefing. The room crackled with a mix of tension and excitement. Everyone here knew the stakes, the risks, and the potential impact of what they were about to do.

"In less than an hour, we launch a coordinated strike against Volkov's organization," Olivia said, her voice calm and resolute. "This is what we've been working towards, what we've sacrificed for. I won't lie to you – it's going to be dangerous. Volkov and his people won't go down without a fight."

She paused, making eye contact with each team member in turn. "But I have faith in every one of you. We've faced betrayal, we've overcome setbacks, and we're going to end Volkov's reign of terror together, stronger than ever."

Jack stepped forward, his face stern but determined. "All strike teams are in position and awaiting your order, Olivia. We're ready to move on your command."

Elena nodded in agreement. "Our international partners are standing by. The moment we give the signal, we'll have a global net closing in on Volkov's entire network."

From her station, Natalie chimed in. "Surveillance systems are at full capacity. We'll have real-time intelligence throughout the operation."

Diego held up his tablet. "The moment we get the green light, we'll start freezing accounts and tracking transactions. Financial task force is ready."

Looking at her team, Olivia felt a surge of pride. Despite everything they'd been through, the personal cost to each of them, they stood united, ready to face whatever challenges lay ahead.

"Alright, people," she said, her voice ringing with authority. "This is it. Everything we've worked for comes down to the next few hours. Stay focused, watch each other's backs, and remember – we're not just fighting for ourselves. We're fighting for every person who's suffered under Volkov's corruption."

She paused, letting her words sink in. Then, with a nod to Jack, she gave the order they'd all been waiting for.

"Let's move out."

As her team sprang into action, Olivia felt a mix of emotions: a fierce hope that they would succeed where others had failed, tempered with anxiety and resolve. The road ahead would be fraught with danger and uncertainty. But as she watched her team's flawless efficiency, Olivia knew that whatever challenges they faced, they would face them together.

The betrayals they had uncovered had shaken them, but they had also sharpened their resolve. Now, united by a common purpose and an unyielding commitment to justice, Olivia Raines and her team were more cohesive than ever as they prepared to strike at the heart of Volkov's empire.

As the first reports of successful raids began to come in, Olivia allowed herself a small smile. They had taken the first crucial steps, though the battle was far from over. Whatever the outcome, she knew this day would mark a turning point in their lives as much as in their mission.

Olivia took a deep breath and focused on the operation at hand. The next few hours would determine the fate of their mission, potentially altering the landscape of international crime. But whatever challenges lay ahead, Olivia Raines was ready to meet them head-on, with her dedicated team by her side.

Chapter 16: The Last Attack

Tension permeated the air of the command center as Olivia Raines called her staff to order. The room fell silent, all eyes riveted on the battle-hardened commander as she stood before a large map displaying Andrei Volkov's fortified hideaway. This was it—the culmination of months of preparation, countless sleepless nights, and sacrifices that had stretched each of them to their breaking point. This was their final attack.

"Listen up, people," Olivia's voice cut through the silence, steady and firm. "We have one shot at this. Volkov's reign ends today."

Elena Salazar stepped forward, her fingers deftly tracing the map's contours. "The fortress is a maze of defensive positions and hidden passages," she said, highlighting key access points. "Our main objectives are here, here, and here." Her hand moved swiftly, indicating three crucial locations within the compound.

Natalie Harper shifted a set of holographic screens, showcasing the latest satellite images and surveillance data. "Confirmed sightings of Volkov and his top lieutenants as of 0600 hours," she reported, her voice tinged with a mix of excitement and apprehension. "They're holed up in the central command post, heavily guarded."

Olivia nodded, her gaze sweeping across her team's faces. To the side, Jack Tanner and Diego Ortega methodically checked their weapons and gear, their determined expressions reflecting the gravity of the task ahead.

"Jack, you'll lead the naval assault," Olivia said, her eyes locking with the seasoned agent. "We need to split their attention and resources; hit them hard and fast from the sea."

Jack nodded grimly, his mind already racing through tactical scenarios. "Understood. We'll give them hell."

"Diego, you're with me on the ground team," Olivia continued. "Once we breach the outer defenses, your expertise in demolitions and close-quarters combat will be crucial."

The former special forces operative flexed his fingers, a focused gleam in his eye. "Just point me in the right direction, boss. I'll clear the path."

As Olivia assigned specific roles to each team member, the weight of the moment settled over the room. Each of them acutely aware of the dangers ahead, they exchanged glances of grim determination. This wasn't just another mission; it was their chance to finally bring down one of the world's most notorious criminals.

"Remember," Olivia added, her voice quieter but no less intense, "we're not just fighting for ourselves. We're fighting for every life Volkov has destroyed, for every family he's torn apart. Failure is not an option."

As final preparations were completed, the team departed under the cover of darkness. While Olivia guided her ground forces with relentless focus, the surrounding forest was dense and unforgiving. Every movement was silent as they navigated the treacherous terrain, each step deliberate.

Jack Tanner and his naval squad cut through the choppy waves, their inflatable boats nearly silent as they approached the rocky shore. Ahead, the fortress loomed, a dark silhouette against the star-studded sky.

"All teams, comms check," Natalie's voice crackled through their earpieces from the mobile command center.

"Ground team, in position," Olivia whispered.

"Naval team, ready to engage," Jack responded.

"Perimeter security located," Diego reported, scouting ahead of the ground team. "Ready to neutralize on your command, Olivia."

Olivia took a deep breath, the air thick with anticipation. This was the moment of truth. "All teams, execute Operation Checkmate. Go, go, go!"

In an instant, the night erupted into chaos. Explosions rocked the front gate and shook the compound as Diego's strategically placed charges detonated. Alarms blared, floodlights blazing to life and cutting through the darkness.

Taking advantage of the confusion, Olivia's team surged forward. Gunfire erupted as Volkov's guards scrambled to mount a defense. The staccato rhythm of automatic weapons and the acrid scent of cordite filled the air.

"Push forward!" Olivia shouted, her voice rising above the din of battle. She led her squad deeper into the compound, moving with fluid grace as each of her shots found its mark.

On the sea, Jack's forces engaged Volkov's naval defenses with equal ferocity. The dark waters lit up with muzzle flashes and explosions as the two forces clashed. Jack's voice remained calm and steady as he directed his team, years of experience evident in every command.

"Target their flagship!" he ordered, eyeing the massive vessel at the center of Volkov's fleet. "Cripple their command and control!"

From the mobile command center, Natalie worked tirelessly as the battle raged on land and sea, her fingers flying over holographic keyboards. "Accessing their security systems now," she reported, her voice taut with concentration. "Expect inner defenses to start failing in three... two... one..."

On cue, security doors began to malfunction, and automated defense systems sputtered and died. Olivia's team seized their advantage, advancing rapidly through the outer layers of the compound.

The resistance they encountered was fierce. Volkov's guards fought with the desperation of men who knew failure meant certain death. But

Olivia's team was a well-oiled machine, each member moving in perfect synchronization.

In close-quarters combat, Jack Tanner was a blur of motion, his fists and combat knife dispatching opponent after opponent. "We're making headway," he grunted into his comm, "but they're putting up one hell of a fight."

Diego Ortega made devastating use of his intimate knowledge of the compound's layout. He seemed to materialize from the shadows, neutralizing key defensive positions before the guards even realized he was there. "Eastern sector cleared," he reported. "Moving to support the main thrust."

From her elevated position, Elena Salazar provided crucial cover fire. Her sniper rifle cracked repeatedly, each shot finding its mark with unerring precision. "Watch your six, Olivia," she warned. "Heavy resistance approaching from the south corridor."

Olivia acknowledged the warning with a terse nod, her mind racing as she assessed the evolving battlefield. Every decision could mean the difference between victory and catastrophic failure. She directed her team with a combination of hand signals and short, sharp commands, utilizing every scrap of cover as they advanced.

The naval battle raged with equal intensity. Jack's team had managed to close in on Volkov's flagship, but the behemoth of a ship was putting up a hellish defense. Tracer fire lit up the night sky, and the thunderous boom of naval guns reverberated across the water.

"We need to take out their main guns!" Jack shouted, his voice barely audible over the cacophony of battle. "Diego, if you've got a clear shot, we could use some help here!"

Diego, hearing the call, broke away from the main group and scaled a guard tower with incredible speed. Setting up his sniper rifle, he took a deep breath, steadying his aim. "I see the gun crews," he stated. "Taking the shot."

A series of precise shots rang out, and suddenly the flagship's main guns fell silent. Jack seized the opportunity, urging his forces to close in for the killing blow. "Plant the charges!" he ordered. "Let's send this monster to the bottom!"

As the naval team executed their daring plan, Olivia's ground forces pushed ever deeper into the heart of Volkov's fortress. The resistance grew more desperate with each passing minute, but so did the team's resolve.

"We're approaching the inner sanctum," Olivia reported, her breath coming in short gasps as she took cover behind a bullet-riddled wall. "Natalie, what's our status?"

"Inner security systems are in disarray," Natalie replied, her voice tense with concentration. "But be careful - I'm detecting some systems that are isolated from the main grid. There could be surprises waiting for you."

Olivia nodded grimly. "Understood. All teams, stay alert. We're in the endgame now."

As if to punctuate her words, a massive explosion shook the complex. For a moment, everyone froze, fearing the worst. Then Jack's triumphant voice came over the comms: "Flagship neutralized! I repeat, Volkov's flagship is going down!"

A cheer went up from the team, but Olivia quickly reined them in. "Celebrate later," she said. "We're not done yet. Push forward!"

The final assault on Volkov's command center was a whirlwind of gunfire, explosions, and hand-to-hand combat. Olivia's team advanced relentlessly, like a force of nature. Elena's precise marksmanship eliminated threats before they could fully materialize, while Diego's explosives breached heavily fortified doors.

At last, after what felt like an eternity of fighting, they stood before the massive doors of Volkov's inner sanctum. The team paused to catch their breath, checking weapons and wounds.

"This is it," Olivia said, her voice quiet but resolute. "Whatever happens in there, know that I couldn't have asked for a better team. Let's finish this."

With a nod to Diego, the doors were breached, and they stormed inside. The scene that greeted them was one of controlled chaos. Andrei Volkov stood at the center, his face a mask of rage and disbelief, flanked by his elite guards.

"Raines!" he roared, his accent thick with fury. "You dare to invade my home?"

Olivia stood tall, her weapon trained on Volkov's chest. "It's over, Andrei. Your empire falls today."

For a brief moment, the room was deathly silent. Then, as if a switch had been flipped, all hell broke loose. Olivia's team scattered, seeking cover where they could as Volkov's guards opened fire.

The final battle was a maelstrom of skill and savagery. Working in tandem, Jack and Diego systematically dismantled Volkov's defenses, their years of experience evident in every move. Elena provided crucial support, her lethal accuracy ringing out whenever a clear line of fire presented itself.

And at the heart of it all was Olivia, locked in a deadly dance with Volkov himself. The crime lord moved with the skill of years of training and hard-won experience, no slouch in combat. But Olivia matched him blow for blow, her determination fueling every strike.

"You're a fool, Raines," Volkov spat as they grappled. "You can't stop what's coming. Even if you take me down, there will always be others to take my place."

Olivia didn't rise to the bait, focusing all her attention on the fight at hand. Beneath his bravado, she could see the fear in Volkov's eyes as he realized his defeat was inevitable.

As the battle raged on, Olivia's team steadily gained the upper hand. One by one, Volkov's top guards fell until at last, it was just Volkov himself, cornered like a wounded animal.

With a final roar of defiance, he lunged at Olivia, a hidden blade glinting in his grasp. But Olivia was ready. She sidestepped his attack, caught his arm, and in one fluid motion, sent him crashing to the ground—a move that seemed almost choreographed.

Volkov struggled, but Olivia quickly secured his hands behind his back. "Andrei Volkov," she declared, her voice ringing with authority, "you are under arrest for crimes against humanity, terrorism, and a list of offenses too long to enumerate. Your reign of terror ends today."

As the sound of incoming helicopters filled the air—reinforcements arriving to secure the facility and its high-value prisoner—Olivia allowed herself a moment to take in the scene. Amidst the wreckage of Volkov's last stand, her battered but triumphant team stood tall.

Jack limped over, a slight hitch in his step but a smile on his face. "Not bad for a day's work, eh boss?"

Olivia found herself grinning. "Not bad at all, Jack. Not bad at all."

As Volkov was led away, Olivia felt a weight lift from her shoulders. Years of her life had been consumed by a mission that had cost the lives of friends and colleagues; it was finally over. Even as relief washed over her, she knew their work was far from done. Volkov's network was vast, and dismantling it would take time and effort.

But as she looked at her team—at Diego's quiet strength, Elena's unwavering focus, Jack's easy confidence, matched by Natalie's sharp intellect—Olivia knew they were equal to the task. Whatever came next, they would face it together.

As the first light of dawn broke over the horizon, painting the sky in hues of pink and gold, Olivia Raines led her team out of the ruined remains of Volkov's fortress. They were more than just victors; they were a message to the criminal underworld: no one was beyond the reach of justice. They were the harbingers of a new era.

The helicopters touched down, kicking up swirls of dust and debris. As Volkov was being escorted away, securely restrained and surrounded by armed guards, Olivia turned to her team. Though their faces showed signs of scratches, bruises, and fatigue, there was a shared look of triumph in their eyes.

"I know I don't say this enough," Olivia said, her voice thick with emotion, "but I'm proud of each and every one of you. What we've accomplished here today... it's going to save countless lives. It's going to give hope to those who had none. Remember this moment. Remember why we do what we do."

Jack nodded solemnly, his arm draped over Diego's shoulder for support. "Wouldn't have missed it for the world, boss."

Elena, her sniper rifle slung across her back, allowed herself a rare grin. "We do make a pretty good team, don't we?"

"The best," Diego affirmed, his usually stoic demeanor softening momentarily.

Natalie emerged from the mobile command center, her face pale from hours of intense concentration, but her eyes shining with victory. "We've got what we need to take down Volkov's entire network. The data we've recovered from his systems is a goldmine."

Olivia nodded, her mind already turning to the work ahead. For now, though, she allowed herself to savor the victory. "Let's go home," she said quietly. "We've earned some rest."

As they boarded the chopper, Olivia cast one last glance at Volkov's crumbling stronghold. In her mind's eye, she saw not just the physical structure falling, but the metaphorical collapse of a criminal empire that had once seemed untouchable. It was a reminder that with dedication, teamwork, and unwavering resolve, even the mightiest adversaries could be brought to justice.

The rotors spun to life, drowning out the last echoes of battle. As they lifted off, Olivia felt a sense of closure, but also of new beginnings. They were leaving behind the site of their greatest triumph, but the world was a little safer today because of their efforts. And tomorrow, they would wake up ready to face whatever challenges lay ahead.

For Olivia Raines and her team, this was more than just a job. It was a calling, a sacred duty. As long as there were threats to face and wrongs to right, they would be there, a beacon against the darkness.

The helicopter banked, heading for home. In the distance, the sun continued its ascent, a fitting symbol for the brighter future they had fought so hard to ensure. Though the battle against tyranny and injustice would go on, this chapter was closed. And surrounded by the finest team Olivia Raines could have wished for, she was ready for whatever came next.

As the coastline receded behind them, Olivia allowed herself a moment of quiet introspection. The weight of leadership had never felt heavier, yet at the same time, she had never been more certain of her path. Today's victory was significant, but it was just one battle in a much larger war. All the lessons learned, the bonds forged in combat, the sacrifices made—they would serve them well in the challenges that lay ahead.

Olivia took a deep breath and then looked forward, toward the horizon and the future it held. Whatever came next, she and her team would face it together, united in their commitment to justice and their unbreakable bond as brothers and sisters in arms.

The helicopter carried them onward, toward home, rest, and the next chapter in their ongoing struggle for a better world.

Epilogue

In the weeks that followed the fall of Andrei Volkov, the ripple effects of their operation were felt across the globe. Criminal networks scrambled to fill the power vacuum, while law enforcement agencies capitalized on the wealth of intelligence gleaned from Volkov's databases.

Olivia and her team worked tirelessly, coordinating with international partners to dismantle what remained of Volkov's empire. Each day brought new challenges, but also new victories. Slowly but surely, they were making a difference.

One evening, as the sun set over the city, Olivia found herself standing on the balcony of their headquarters. The weight of responsibility still rested heavily on her shoulders, but there was a newfound lightness to her step.

"Penny for your thoughts, boss?" Jack's voice came from behind her.

Olivia turned, offering a small smile to her old friend. "Just thinking about how far we've come. And how far we still have to go."

Jack nodded, leaning against the railing beside her. "We've done good, Liv. Real good. But you're right—there's always more to do."

"Do you ever wonder if it's enough?" Olivia asked, her voice quiet. "If we're really making a difference in the grand scheme of things?"

Jack was silent for a moment, his gaze sweeping over the city below. "I think," he said slowly, "that every life we save, every criminal we put away, every bit of hope we give to people—it all adds up. We might not change the whole world overnight, but we're changing it bit by bit, day by day."

Olivia nodded, feeling a surge of gratitude for her team, for their unwavering support and shared commitment to their cause.

"Besides," Jack added with a grin, "someone's got to keep the bad guys up at night. Might as well be us."

Olivia chuckled, the sound light and genuine. "I suppose you're right."

As if on cue, Natalie's voice came over the intercom. "Team, we've got a situation developing in Eastern Europe. Briefing in five."

Olivia and Jack exchanged a look, a mix of determination and excitement passing between them. The world needed them, and they were ready to answer the call.

"Well," Olivia said, straightening up, "duty calls."

As they headed back inside, Olivia felt a renewed sense of purpose. The road ahead would be challenging, filled with dangers and difficult choices. But with her team by her side, she was ready to face whatever came their way.

The fight for justice was never-ending, but Olivia Raines and her team were in it for the long haul. They were the guardians in the shadows, the protectors of the innocent, the bearers of hope in a world that often seemed consumed by darkness.

And as long as there were those who sought to harm and exploit others, Olivia and her team would be there, standing strong against the tide of evil, ready to make a difference—one mission at a time.

The End

Milton Keynes UK
Ingram Content Group UK Ltd.
UKHW030344240824
447344UK00001BA/110

9 798227 893826